Edgar tried to finish the story, to give it a proper ending, and seal away the shadows, but as he worked, the images faded. He fought a losing battle with his mind for control of the words. He heard the loud flutter of wings. He saw the dead man's blood, seeping into the ground. He saw a woman's startled face, and a drawing, a tree, and then a stream of faces, one after the other, roaring directly at him and dissipating to smoke as they brushed his eyelashes.

And then—as suddenly as it all began—it was gone. He sat stunned, staring at the scratched, torn paper on the table and the ruined, brutalized tip of his pen. Grimm was nowhere to be seen, and from what seemed very far away, he heard a woman's cry, and the crash of something falling.

Everything I write, and everything I do, begins with thanks to the Elder Gods, all of them who have visited me in my dreams and blessed me in my life with the love and support of Patricia Lee Macomber. She helped me edit this, listened to me go on about if at length, and it could not have happened without her.
Special thanks, as well, to my kids for their patience, and our pets for possibly the most unselfish love mankind ever encounters…
And thank you to my friends, and colleagues, Kurt Criscione, keeper of the DeChance Bible, David Dodd, friend and business partner and wizard of spreadsheets and databases.
Finally—to my muse, I tip a tumbler of bourbon to you, old friend. We did it again.

# NEVERMORE

*A Tale of Love, Loss, & Edgar Allan Poe*

## DAVID NIALL WILSON

*I want to dedicate this book to Edgar Allan Poe, the real man, the man I imagined, the poet, and the dreamer. I will also dedicate it to Lenore—the lost love, the mystery woman, and to the heart of that wonderful enigma, The Great Dismal Swamp.*

# A Dream Within A Dream

Take this kiss upon the brow!
And, in parting from you now,
Thus much let me avow—
You are not wrong, who deem
That my days have been a dream;
Yet if hope has flown away
In a night, or in a day,
In a vision, or in none,
Is it therefore the less gone?
All that we see or seem
Is but a dream within a dream.

I stand amid the roar
Of a surf-tormented shore,
And I hold within my hand
Grains of the golden sand—
How few! yet how they creep
Through my fingers to the deep,
While I weep—while I weep!
O God! can I not grasp
Them with a tighter clasp?
O God! can I not save
One from the pitiless wave?
Is all that we see or seem
But a dream within a dream?

—Edgar Allan Poe

# Prologue

The Great Dismal swamp stretches miles and miles back from the long, man-made ditch known as the Intercoastal Waterway. The original idea was that the swamp would be logged, and then drained a section at a time to clear the land. While the logging was a great success, the draining of that ancient, primeval place was far more difficult than anyone had imagined. Engineers and investors gave up, and took to shipping lumber up and down the length of the New World via the waterway, passing all manner of barges, sailboats, and passengers from Florida across the Virginia border.

In 1829, directly on the border of North Carolina and Virginia, The Lake Drummond Hotel was built. This hotel was unique, resting half in one state, and half in the other, with a tavern in the very center. It lay only a short distance from the banks of the waterway, and not far from the shoreline of Lake Drummond, which was already famous in local legend.

The lake is a dark, mystical place. The poet Thomas Moore wrote a ballad about the ghost of a young Indian maiden who died near Lake Drummond, just before her wedding, and how her lover came to the lake, looking for her in vain. Her ghost is still said to haunt the swamp, appearing now and then, paddling a canoe, or walking out into the water.

There is a tree there so closely shaped like a deer that legend has it a witch was fleeing pursuit and turned herself into a deer for greater speed. When she found herself trapped by the lake, she transformed a second time—into a tree. This transformation trapped her and she remained by the side of the lake, her deer form captured in the warped cypress forever.

The Lake Drummond Hotel stood from 1829 until about 1840. It was famous for advertising itself as a place appropriate for drinking, dueling, trysts, and a wide-variety of shady deals. The marriage laws in North Carolina were a lot more lenient than those of Virginia. A duel, held across the state lines, one duelist on either side, presented difficulties for those prosecuting from either side of the line. Along with this, traffic up and down the waterway brought those fleeing, and those chasing, across multiple state lines.

Famous people found their way in and out of the Lake Drummond Hotel. Edgar Allan Poe almost certainly wrote his poem, "The Lake," about Lake Drummond. He traveled through after his somewhat storied military career came to an end, and before his writing really brought him the beginnings of the small fame and fortune he achieved during his lifetime.

Every story has roots in reality. Lake Drummond, and the hotel, spawned thousands. This is only one.

# Chapter One

The room was low-ceilinged and deep. Smoke wafted from table to table, cigars, pipes, and the pungent aroma of scented candles. Laughter floated out from the bar, separated by a low half-wall from a small dining area, where the bartender regaled the crowd with a particularly bawdy story. In the corners, more private conversations took place, and at the rear, facing the Intercoastal Waterway beyond, the door stood open to the night, letting the slightly cooler air of evening in and the sound and smoke free.

The smoke prevented the illumination from a series of gaslights and lanterns from cutting the gloom properly. Smiles gleamed from shadows and the glint of silver and gunmetal winked like stars. It was a rough crowd, into their drinks and stories, plans and schemes.

Along the back wall, facing a window that looked out over the waterway and the Great Dismal Swamp beyond, a lone figure sat with her back to the room. Her hair was long and light brown, braided back and falling over her shoulder to the center of her back. She was tall and slender with smooth, tanned skin. She was dressed for travel, in a long, floor length dress that covered her legs, while allowing ease of motion. The crowd swirled around her, but none paid her any attention.

She paid no attention to anything but the window. Her gaze was fixed on the point where an intricate pattern of branches and leaves crossed the face of the moon.

There was a sheaf of paper on the table, and she held a bit of charcoal loosely between the thumb and index finger of her right hand. She formed the trees, the long strong lines of the trees, the fine mesh of branches and mist. Her fingers moved quickly, etching outlines and shading onto her sketch with practiced ease.

A serving girl wandered over to glance down at the work in progress. She stared at the paper intently, and then glanced up at the window, and the night beyond. She reached down and plucked the empty wine glass from the table.

"What are they?" she asked.

The woman glanced up. Her expression was startled, as if she'd been drawn back from some other place, or out of a trance. She followed the serving girl's gaze to the paper.

Among the branches, formed of limbs and leaves, mist and reflected light, faces gazed out, some at the tavern, some at the swamp, others down along the waterway. They mixed so subtly with the trees themselves that if you were not looking carefully, they seemed to disappear.

"I don't know," the woman said. "Not yet. Spirits, I suppose. Trapped. Tangled."

"You are a crazy woman," the girl said. There was no conviction in her words. She continued to stare at the sketch. Then, very suddenly, she stepped back. She stumbled, and nearly dropped her tray.

The woman glanced up at her sharply.

"What?"

"That…face." The girl stepped back to the table very slowly, and pointed to the center of the snarl of branches. The tip of her finger brushed along the lines of a square-jawed face. The eyes were dark and the expression was a scowl close to rage.

"I've seen him before," she said. "Last year. He…he was shot."

"Can you tell me?"

The girl shook her head. "Not now. I have to work. If I stand here longer there will be trouble. Later? I must serve until the tavern closes, a few hours…"

The artist held out her hand.

"My Name is Eleanor, Eleanor MacReady, but friends call me Lenore. I'll be here, finishing this drawing, until you close. I know that it will be late, but I am something of a night person. Can we talk then? Maybe in my room?"

The girl nodded. She glanced down at the drawing again and stepped back. Then she stumbled off into the crowded tavern and disappeared. Lenore stared after her for a long moment, brow furrowed, then turned back to the window. The moon had shifted, and the image she'd been drawing was lost. It didn't matter. The faces were locked in her mind, and she turned her attention to her wine glass, and to the paper. The basic design was complete, but there was a lot of shading and detail work remaining. She had to get the faces just right—exactly as she remembered them. Then the real work would begin.

Even as she worked, her mind drifted out toward the swamp, and toward her true destination. She didn't know the exact location of the tree, but she knew it was there, and she knew that she would find it. She didn't always see things in her dreams, but when she did, the visions were always true.

A breeze blew in through the open window, and she shivered.

The face she was working on was that of an older man. He had a sharp, beak of a nose and deep-set shadowed eyes. The expression on his face might have been surprise, or dismay. His hair was formed of strands of gray cloud blended with small twigs and wisps of fog as she carefully entered the details.

There were others. She'd counted five in all, just in that one glimpse of the swamp. She thought she could probably sit right here, at this window, and work for years without capturing them all. How many lives lay buried in the peat moss and murky water? How many had died, or been killed beside the long stretch of the Intercoastal Waterway? She tilted her head and listened. The breeze seemed to carry voices from far away, the sound of firing guns, the screams of the lost and dying.

She worked a woman's features into a knotted joint in one of the tree's branches. The face was proud. Her lip curled down slightly at the edge, not so much in a frown, as in determination. Purpose. From the strong cheekbones and distinctive lines of the woman's nose, Lenore sensed she'd been an Indian. How had she come here, soul trapped fluttering up through the sticky fingers of the ancient trees?

Around her, the sounds of revelry, arguments of drunken, belligerent men, clink of glasses, full and empty, and the sound of a lone guitar in a far corner surrounded her. She felt cut off—isolated in some odd way from everyone, and everything but the paper beneath her fingers. Now and then she paused, reached out for her glass, and sipped her wine.

No one troubled her and that in and of itself, was odd. A woman—an attractive woman—alone in a place like the Halfway House was an oddity. She should have been a target. She was not. A few men glanced her way, but something about her—the way she bent over her work, the intensity of her focus—kept them away. She worked steadily, and one by one, the others drifted out the doors, some to rooms, others to wander about with bottles and thoughts of their own. Eventually, there were only a few small groups, talking quietly, the bartender, and the girl.

There was nothing more she could do. She had drawn an eerily accurate re-creation of the trees over the waterway, and of the five faces she'd found trapped in their branches. She sensed things about them but knew little. She did not need to know. She knew that she had to set them free, to allow them to move on to the next level. Something had bound them—some power, or some part of themselves they were unwilling to release. They did not belong, and though she knew that most of the world either ignored, or did not sense these things at all—she did. All those trapped, helpless beings weighed on her spirit like stones. She was fine until she saw them, but once that happened, she was bound to set them free. It was her gift— her curse? Sometimes the two were too closely aligned to be differentiated.

She rose, drained the last of the wine in her cup, and gathered her pencils. She tucked the drawing into the pocket of a leather portfolio, careful not to smudge it. Soon, it would not matter, but until she'd had a chance to finish her work, it was crucial that nothing be disturbed.

The girl, who had been busy wiping the spilled remnants of ale, wine, and the night from the various tables and the surface of the bar, wandered slowly over.

"I'm in the corner room," Lenore said, smiling. "The one farthest in on the Carolina side."

The girl nodded. She glanced over at the bartender, then turned back.

"I will come as soon as I can." She glanced down at the portfolio. "You have finished?"

Lenore nodded, but only slightly. "I have finished the basic drawing, yes."

"He was a bad man," the girl said. "A very bad man. I have never seen him there—in the trees—before tonight. I don't like that he watches."

"After tonight, he will not," Lenore said, reaching to lay her hand on the girl's shoulder. "But I'd love to know who he is—who he was. I seldom know the faces I've drawn. You saw him—in my drawing, and in the trees. Most see nothing but branches."

"I will come soon," the girl said, turning and hurrying back toward the bar.

Lenore watched her go, frowned slightly, and then turned. She had to exit through the front door and follow a long porch along the side of the building where it turned from the saloon in the center to a line of rooms on the Carolina side. There were similar rooms on the Virginia side, but her business was in the swamp, and the corner room gave her a better view of what lay beyond.

As she made her way to her room, she heard the steady drum of hooves. She stopped and turned. A carriage had come into view, winding in from the main road that stretched between the states. It was dark, pulled by a pair of even darker horses. She stood still and watched as it came to a halt. Something moved far above, and she glanced up in time to see a dark shape flash across the pale face of the moon. A bird? At night?

She glanced back to the carriage to see it pulling away into the night. A single figure stood, his bag in one hand. He glanced her way, nodded, and then turned toward the main door of the saloon. He was thin, with dark hair and eyes. It was hard to make his features out in the darkness, but somehow she saw into those eyes. They were filled with an odd, melancholy sadness. As he passed inside, it seemed as if his shadow remained, just for a moment, outlined in silvery light. Then it was gone.

Lenore shook her head, turned, and hurried to the door to her room. She fumbled the key from her jacket pocket, jammed it into the lock, and stepped inside. She had no idea why the sight of the man had unnerved her, but it had. And the bird. If she'd woken from a dream, she'd have believed she was meant to set him free…but she was very, very awake, and though her fingers itched to draw—to put his image on paper and tuck it away somewhere safe, she knew she could not. Not now—not yet. There was not much time before dawn, and she still had work to finish—and a story to hear. The stranger, if she ever returned to him, would have to wait.

She lit the oil lamp on the single table in her small room, opened the portfolio, and laid the drawing on the flat surface. There was a small stand nearby, and another bottle of wine rested there. She had two glasses, but had not known at the time why she'd asked for them. Another vision? She poured one for herself, and replaced the cork.

Moments later, there was a soft rap on the door. When she opened it, the girl stood outside, shifting nervously from one foot to the other and looking up and down the long porch as if fearing to be seen.

"Come in," Lenore said.

The girl did so, and Lenore closed the door behind them.

"What shall I call you?" she asked, trying to set the girl at ease. Something had her spooked and it would simply not do to have the girl bolt without spilling her story.

"Anita," the girl said shyly, glancing at Lenore. "I am Anita."

"I'm glad to meet you," Lenore said, "and very curious to hear what you have to say about the man you saw in the trees. I see them all the time, you know. In trees, bushes, sometimes in the water or a stone. It's not very often that I meet another who is aware of them—even less often that I have a chance to hear their stories."

"It is not a good story," Anita said. "He was a very bad man."

Lenore smiled again. "He's not a man any longer, dear, so there is nothing to fear in the telling. Would you like a glass of wine?"

The girl nodded. Lenore poured a second glass from her bottle and handed it over.

"Sit down," she said. "I still have work to do, and I can work as you talk. It will relax me."

"I will tell you," Anita said, perching lightly on the corner of the bed, "but it will not relax you."

"Then it will keep me awake," Lenore said, seating herself at her desk. "You see, I don't just see those who are trapped, I have to undo whatever it is that has them trapped. I won't be finished until I've freed them all."

The girl glanced sharply over, nearly spilling her drink.

"Maybe…maybe it is best if this one stays."

Lenore pulled out her pencils, and a gum eraser.

"We'll leave him for now," she said. "There are four others, and I can only work on one at a time. Tell me your story."

Anita took a sip of her wine, and nodded. "His name was Abraham Thigpen. He died about a year ago but I remember it like today…"

Lenore listened, and worked, rearranging branches, shifting the wood slightly, picking the strong woman's face to release from the pattern first. Anita's voice droned in the background—and she faded into the story, letting it draw her back across the years as she carefully disassembled her drawing, working the faces free.

# Chapter Two

The carriage pulled away, heading back to the main road and on into the plantations of southern Virginia. Edgar watched it for a moment, wishing he were continuing on, and then turned toward the main door of the Halfway House. He'd written ahead for a room, but had not been in Raleigh long enough to wait for a reply. Besides, the Lake Drummond Hotel was not the sort of place that catered to amenities such as reservations. You could let them know you were coming, but there was literally no way of knowing what you'd walk into when you arrived.

The tavern was nearly empty when he stepped inside. There was a young boy sweeping the floor, and behind the bar, an older man with well-combed gray hair and a silver mustache who was placing dried and polished glasses on the shelves. The man turned as Edgar entered.

"We're closed, I'm afraid," he said.

"I'm here for a room?" Edgar said. He stepped forward. "I wrote ahead. I'm hoping you aren't full, as I need to remain for several days, if possible."

The bartender dropped his towel on the bar and smiled.

"Ah," he said. "Mr. Poe. We were expecting you, but I thought you'd arrive tomorrow in the day. We held a room for you, the last empty room available. I was beginning to regret not renting it."

Edgar let out a breath. "Thank you for holding it," he said. "I'm afraid I don't have any way to leave, so I took something of a chance."

"Tom," the bartender called to the boy with the broom. "Show Mr. Poe to his room—it's the one right next to the corner, beside Miss MacReady's quarters. And mind you, don't make too much noise. The hour is late, and I imagine she's gone off to sleep."

"Not that one," the boy said. He grinned. "She's up all hours—seen the light from her window on my way home a couple'a times."

The bartender frowned. "Never you mind that," the man said. "Do as you're told. And speaking of home, run off when you're done. I don't want you missing an hour's sleep and playing the slacker come tomorrow."

"Yessir," the boy replied. "Come on, Mister."

He turned on his heel and hurried toward the door, as if afraid he'd be summoned back after all to wash another pile of dirty dishes, or mop the floor a second time. Edgar nodded to the bartender and followed Tom out into the darkness. As he stepped outside he heard the soft rustle of feathers, and he smiled. He did not look up, but instead turned down the porch.

Tom had grabbed a key on his way out of the tavern. He unlocked the door to the room, and then handed it over. "There's a lantern in there," he said. "Should be a coal in the fire too, if you poke at it."

"Thank you, Tom," Edgar said. "Am I to understand that you live on a farm?"

The boy nodded. "I got four brothers and two sisters, all older. They do most of the farming. Pa hired me on here to do odd jobs and clean up. Said I was always 'underfoot'."

"I wonder if you might do me a favor, then," Edgar said. He reached into his pocket and pulled out a copper penny. "I wonder if you might bring me a bit of corn."

The boy stared at the penny, then glanced up at Edgar as if certain he was talking to a crazy man.

"Corn?" he asked.

"Corn," Edgar affirmed. "I am partial to birds, you see. I like to feed them, and I find that if I drop a handful of corn outside my window they gather very regularly. Can you do this for me?"

Tom snatched the coin and grinned.

"You bet," he said.

"I thank you," Edgar said. The boy turned and hurried off into the night, as though afraid Edgar would ask for the money back.

With a chuckle and glance to the empty sky, Edgar entered his room. He left the door open a crack until he'd located the lantern. He lit it with practiced ease, turning the wick up just slightly to increase the flame's brightness. Then he returned to the door. He closed it and locked it carefully, then laid his bag on one of the two wooden chairs and pulled it open.

The room had a small chest of drawers along the side wall, and he carefully unpacked and stored his clothing. Next he pulled out the book he was reading, a novella titled Carmen, by Prosper Mérimée, and his worn copy of Children's and Household Tales—or—Grimm's Fairy Tales. He set these aside almost without thought and drew forth a thick sheaf of papers bound in a ribbon, his pens, and a small bottle of ink. He glanced at the window. Through the curtains he saw that there was a light. He placed the ink, pens, and paper on the table that rested against the wall beneath the window and pulled the curtain aside curiously.

To the right, along the back of the building and on toward the tavern, only the moonlight shone down to illuminate the trees lining the near side of the Intercoastal Waterway. To the left, however, at the very corner of the building, flickering lamplight danced outside the window of the room adjacent to his.

What had the tavern keeper said? Miss MacReady? And the boy, Tom? "She's up all hours…"

It seemed that it was true. Edgar smiled. He was no stranger to late nights. He sometimes believed he would be unable to write at all if it were not for the long hours between dusk and dawn, when the world quieted, after a fashion, the light flickered, the paper took on a yellow lamp-light hue, and his imagination wandered. He thought of his desk, and his home—and that brought him to thoughts of his wife, Virginia, and her failing health.

He turned abruptly back to the chair and opened a side-pocket on his bag. He pulled free a large, silver-plated flask and carried it to the table. The wind was picking up outside, blowing in from the south. Trees swayed, and the roaring throaty breath of the storm teased along the walls and through the slats of the roof. It was a proper night for writing, and only the words—and the whiskey—could draw him up and out of the cloud of despair that was his constant traveling companion.

Virginia was always on his mind. Theirs had been a troubled relationship from the beginning, their familial ties, and the girl's age, but he'd seen something in her—some fragile beauty—that completed him. Now—having filled the hole in his heart, she withered, and he felt the pain like a fist squeezing the light from his world.

If only she'd listen to him. If only the things he knew—the things he could do—could ease her pain. There were curatives—elixirs—potions and charms. He knew he could restore her health, but she would not allow it. Not at what she considered to be the cost of her soul. Not if it meant becoming part and parcel to the powers that swam through the darker recesses of his mind. It was likely that she had trouble deciding if he were evil, or simply mad.

He knew that, despite her wishes, he could save her, but if he did, she would hate him. She would not be happy, and making her happy was all that he craved. Instead, she died, and he drank, and he wrote and he prayed that when all the smoke and dust had cleared that something of worth would remain.

A dark shape dropped through the light from the MacReady woman's lantern. Edgar walked to the window, glanced out, and actually smiled. He unfastened the sash and lifted the window a crack. The scents of blooming flowers and impending storm wafted in. He lifted the window a bit farther, and with a hop, a large crow landed on the windowsill, then dropped into the room with a thud. It sat glaring at him for a moment, and then, as if satisfied in some way, began to busily and noisily preen its feathers.

"Good evening, Grimm." Edgar said with a slight, mock bow. "And it is good to see you too. Perhaps I shall groom my mustache while you are busy, as a show of camaraderie?"

The bird glanced up at him, and then continued working over its tail feathers in complete indifference.

Edgar closed the window and took a seat at the table. He arranged his papers carefully, gathering those he'd written the night before on top of a larger stack of blank sheets. He always began by re-reading what he'd just finished. It served as a quick pre-edit, and it dropped him back into the story with a fresh 'reader's' perspective of the work.

"Perhaps," he said conversationally, "I shall write a story about a bird—a great black one who is too often inattentive. Grave things might happen to such a creature, don't you think?"

The crow didn't even bother to glance up at this. Edgar chuckled, and turned to the pages before him. He had meant to write a story of romance and intrigue, but as he read, he saw that—once again—the melancholy that served as his muse had taken over and driven dark spikes between the pages. It was clear that one lover must die at the hand of the other, and that the mystery would depend on the circumstances. The young man in the story was quite mad—as was so often the case—mad and absolutely brilliant. Misunderstood. Lonely.

He opened the flask and took a long pull, letting the fiery warmth of it roll back over his tongue and down through the chilly expanse of his heart. Grimm hopped to the tabletop in a flurry of wings. He turned and glared at Edgar again, looking for all the world as if he would snatch the flask and fly off with it. It was Edgar's turn to ignore the bird.

"Leave it be, old friend," Edgar said. "Now is not the time. You are right to disapprove, but I can't help myself. Rather, knowing the pain that it would bring, I will not help myself."

Then, opening the small bottle of ink, he dipped the first of his quills and began to write, dropping away into the world of the story as if it might erase the real world entirely. He told himself the protagonist's pain was not his own, so it was cathartic to pretend that the darkness in his characters' lives was also not his own, and to drive them deeper and deeper until what he suffered in his silence seemed smaller in comparison.

And there were the visions. As he wrote, his mind stretched. It was the only way he could describe it. He reached out to the world beyond him, linked himself to the minds and dreams of others, plucked out the things that frightened them, and made them his own. His mind blended with that of the crow as well, named Grimm for the fairy tales so well-penned by long-dead brothers. The two had traveled together, albeit in secret, for several years. The old bird lent him strength, sometimes wisdom, and more often than not the necessary inspiration to bring another tale to life.

This time it was different. Something had shifted, or changed. He could not drop into the story he was working on properly. He knew what was happening, knew what he thought must come next. He even had bits and pieces of prose handy that he felt he might make use of in the course of recording that particular vision. He could not write it. It had all disappeared from his mind like a puff of smoke. In its place—all he saw were trees.

# Chapter Three

Once she started, Lenore worked steadily. The work that she did was demanding. Once she slipped back into the drawing, she had to remain there, at least until whichever trapped spirit she'd chosen to draw was absolutely freed of the object that trapped it. She tried to think of the spirits as things, and not as the men and women that they had been. Sometimes it was difficult. She felt Anita watching, and waiting. The girl seemed to understand instinctively, that Lenore needed to concentrate, and how important it was. On the other hand, perhaps she was merely gathering her courage before speaking.

The woman's face that Lenore was working with was not difficult. The tree held her, but it did not grip her. Lenore removed a branch carefully with the gum eraser. As she removed one bit of the image, she recreated the details beneath. In her mind, she held a clear vision of the woman as she'd been—as she'd lived. She brushed the twigs and leaves carefully from the lines of the dark hair and filled in the highlights, carefully traced the dark strands across the bisecting wooden cage that held them. It was quick work, but very intense, and when she finished—when she applied the final line beneath the woman's lovely, dark eyes, she heard a gasp behind her.

Instinctively, she pulled the pencil away from the paper, afraid that she might mar the work she'd completed. She turned, and saw that Anita was staring at a point about a foot above the paper. Her eyes were wide, and her mouth wider—she looked as if she might be on the verge of screaming. Lenore's heart quickened. Was it possible?

"Anita!" she said. "What is it? What's wrong?"

"I saw..." the girl shook her head and stepped back. "I saw her...leave."

Lenore stared. In all the years she'd worked the images, perfected her art—in all the time she'd labored to set them free, no other had ever seen. Many had examined and praised her art—the finished pieces hung in some very famous homes across the country, and even in Europe. Others had been able to see what she saw in the trees and stones, mountains and even—at times—water and clouds. Until this moment, though, no one that she'd encountered had ever seen the spirits themselves.

For Lenore, it was a silver, luminescent thread. When she released them, when the final bond with the paper and the image was severed, the end attached to the paper frayed. It split and snapped with tiny pops of light and energy. It unraveled slowly at first, then faster and faster, until suddenly—it broke free. That instant was so fleeting, so quick in its passing, that she often wondered if she imagined the whole thing. She'd been called crazy more than once. Particularly when she was younger, before she'd learned to keep the visions to herself, and only present her art to the outside world.

"What did you see?" she asked. She rose, stepped closer to Anita and reached out to offer support.

"I…I'm not sure," Anita said. "It was…like smoke, but not exactly. Silver. I saw silver, tied to your paper. It unraveled and the colors…oh the colors. It was like a rainbow. Like nothing I've ever seen."

"She is free now," Lenore said.

She led Anita to the other chair, across from her.

"I need to do the same for the others. As I work, I need you to talk to me. Watch, if you will—I have never shared this with another—but talk to me. Tell me the stories you know of this man—this bad one—that you fear. Tell me what it is you know, and I will show you my art, whether it's a gift or a curse you can decide for yourself. Know that when I set him free, the word freedom is a relative one. He is trapped here in this world—in this existence—but he is no longer part of it. He should have passed on to the light, or to the dark, but he should not be here. He is trapped. When I release him, whatever fate he originally earned will be his. He will not be free to harm you, or any other. If it is proper, he will be judged."

Anita stared at the picture. The Indian woman's features were bold and bright. Her eyes gleamed. The likeness was so real, so perfect, that it seemed she might turn her face and smile at them.

Lenore returned to her seat, and Anita took the chair opposite her. She composed herself, ordered her thoughts, and then she began to speak.

"His name was Thigpen. Abraham Thigpen. He was supposed to be a lawman. That is what he said when he took a room. No one questioned him. He was well dressed, and armed. He had a badge. I remember that it shone like silver, and he wore it on the lapel of a long, dark jacket. He said that he was tracking a man—a dangerous man. Again, no one doubted him. This is a place that attracts shadows."

Anita paused. She glanced at Lenore, but got no response. The eraser brushed lightly at the drawing, dragging aside a clump of leaves. The pencil dropped to the paper, and the line of a man's nose was joined where the leaves had been. There were still twigs crossing the man's chin, and a final leaf tangled in his hair to be changed. Anita continued.

"He stayed here almost a week. He was an arrogant man, and crude. The longer he stayed, the more he drank, and each night he grew closer to losing control. I remember him because…"

Anita paused again. Lenore wanted to glance up. She was aware of the story, aware of the words, and she sensed the pain behind them, but she could not allow herself to be distracted. Anita would have to continue in her own time.

"…he tried to have his way with me. I work in the tavern, but that is all. I serve drinks. I clean up. Sometimes, if they need me to, I cook, or tend to the rooms. There are other women—there are always other women. They are here for the men—to take their money and offer…what I do not. This man, this Abraham Thigpen, did not respect this. He put his hands on me again, and again. I asked him to stop. Others asked him, and then told him, but he would not be denied. He believed that I was toying with him; that is what he said. He told me that he was a lawman from a very big city, and that he had seen women like me before—holding out—playing hard to get.

"I am engaged to be married. My fiancé Roberto does not come to the tavern. It is a hard thing for him. He does not like that I have to work, and he does not like that I work so closely beside drunken men. One night, against my wishes, he came to see me. He must have sensed that I was upset, that something was not right. It was a night when this man—Thigpen—was drinking too much ale. He stood by the bar; trying to tell stories of the men he'd brought to justice. I think that by this time, the other men had started to wonder how long he would remain—and why he was not out in the world, bringing more men to justice.

"I was doing my best to ignore Roberto, who sat at a table in the corner. He had ordered beer, and he was not used to drinking it. It was a very busy night. To make my way through the crowd I had to come very close to many customers. Sometimes I brushed against them. Sometimes they joked, or reached for me. It is part of my job—not a part that I enjoy. Roberto did not understand, and he grew angry.

"Then I had to serve ale to Abraham Thigpen. He was already very drunk. His eyes did not seem to focus on me, but on some point behind me, and his words—though directed at me—barely made sense. I brought his drink and turned to leave, but despite being drunk, he moved very quickly.

"He stood, and put his arm around me. Before I knew it he had spun me around, groping me with his hands…and his tongue. I pushed away, but he was strong. I slapped him as hard as I could, but he did not release me. No one moved to stop him, and I was afraid.

"Then Roberto was there. Before I knew what had happened, he was at my side, and Thigpen was staggering back. I remember there was blood; the man held his hand to his face. Roberto wanted to follow and attack him, but I managed to wrap myself around him and hold him back.

"By this time everyone was moving and shouting. Men held Thigpen back, and others grabbed Roberto and pulled me away."

Anita fell silent for a moment, and then continued. Her voice was lower, and it was thick with new emotion.

"Roberto is not a rich man," she said. "He works on one of the farms. He migrated here with his family—we are treated little better than slaves. I have good work here, but…

"They took Roberto away. They took him down to the road, and several men—men I'd served drinks and meals to, beat him. They left him by the trail, and remained close by to be certain he did not return.

"This Thigpen, he grew very cold, and very quiet. He did not scream at me…he talked to the owner of the tavern. I am not sure what he said, but it must have been a threat. They gave him more to drink, and I was called aside. I was told…I was told that if I did not go to that man's rooms and treat him well, I would no longer have a job—and Roberto would be arrested.

"When I asked why—when I begged that it not be so, I was told that Roberto had struck a lawman. That his life should be forfeit and that I should be glad—proud—that I had the chance to redeem him."

Lenore listened, her grip tightening on the pencil and the eraser as the story whirled slowly into darker and darker shadows. Though she worked as she always had, something felt different. She hurriedly finished the details on a young man whose features she'd exhumed from the lines and whirls of the tree's bark. She felt the soft rush of his escape. She did not even glance at the others, but moved straight to the image of the man she now knew as Abraham Thigpen.

Of all the faces she'd found, his was buried most deeply. She started at his chin, working her way up one shade and angle at a time. She was not ready to meet the gaze of his eyes, even dead and spirit trapped in the swamp. She had never known them, those that she drew. Not before they were free—almost never after, though a few had been recognized over the years. Good, bad, whatever, she didn't know them and now this. Now this—evil—so close beneath her fingers, so intertwined with her mind. The words continued—as if in some way Anita had been drawn into the process.

Something dark—with wings—flashed across the periphery of her vision. There was a sound—like a thud—but it floated to her from far away, and though she thought it might be important, she couldn't concentrate on it. The walls blurred. The room faded. Her fingers worked, and she was aware of the work, but she did not see the image. Anita's story claimed her, and suddenly she stood outside herself—outside the tavern—on the long wooden porch that led down the front of the building.

Ahead of her, a tall man lurched drunkenly down the North Carolina side of the Halfway House. He held a girl—Anita—by the wrist, dragging her after him. Lenore tried to move toward them—tried to call out. She could not. She was there, but at the same time, she was not.

"Please," Anita sobbed, pulling back against Thigpen's grip. "Please do not do this. I want to go home."

The man turned, and Lenore saw his eyes flash a bright blue—cold, like chips of ice.

"Shut your mouth, girl," he said. "You will do exactly what I say, or your new home will be a place far from here. There are jails for women like you—places where you could be locked away and forgotten. Your man, as well. He attacked me—I could have him killed."

"Please," she said—softer. She no longer fought, and he ignored her. He stopped by one of the doors, fumbled in his pocket, and produced a key. He was obviously drunk, but it did not seem to prevent him from functioning—a sure sign of a man more used to spirits than sobriety. An odd way for a man of the law to behave.

He dragged Anita through the door, and slammed it closed behind him. Lenore tried, again, to cry out. She moved as if to follow, but the world shifted once again, and she found herself suddenly inside the room. She had not moved, but the world shifted, and she was there.

Anita lay sprawled across the bed. Thigpen stood over her, leering. In one hand he held a flask. With the other, he began to unbutton his shirt, letting it fall open to reveal a chest matted with thick, dark hair. His face—the same face from the image she'd drawn—was dark and filled with lust. He tipped back the flask.

"Take off your clothes, girl," he said. "Take them off now, or I will be forced to do it for you. I assure you, I will enjoy that, if it is necessary, but they will come off."

Anita was crying. Her hair was a mess, and she looked like a crumpled flower. She wore a long, dark skirt, and a white blouse. She gripped the bottom of the blouse, sliding it slowly up. Thigpen stood, wavering from side to side, and watching. He tipped the flask again, took a long drink, and must have emptied it, because he tossed it aside. He staggered toward the bed, reached for the next button on his shirt, and tried to take another step forward.

The alcohol was stronger than he'd imagined, or perhaps he'd just been too far gone to notice. As he neared the bed, his feet became tangled. He fell toward the bed so quickly that Anita had to scramble aside, dropping to the floor, to avoid having him land on her. She scrambled across the rough planks until she came up against the wall, then she turned back, hands flat on the floor, ready to press up and run.

There was no need. Thigpen had fallen face-flat on the bed. He was not moving, and after a long moment, deep snores filled the air. Anita sat very still, drawing one hand up to her breast. She listened...but there was nothing. Very slowly, she pressed off the floor and stood. She crossed the room to the door at a run, turned, and stopped with her hand on the doorknob.

She hesitated then, but Thigpen did not move. With a soft cry, she opened the door and fled into the night, not looking back.

Lenore thought that the vision would end then—but what happened surprised her. The vision shifted. Instead of returning her to her mind, and her work, the lighting changed. When Anita fled the room, it had been very dark outside the door. Moments later, at least it seemed moments, sunlight filtered in through the crack where the girl had left the door ajar, and through the window across the room. She saw motes of dust floating in the air, and in the distance she heard a cock's crow.

Heavy steps sounded on the wood outside. The door was already open, and someone pushed it wide, roughly. Sunlight poured in, but Thigpen did not move.

"Abraham Thigpen!" a voice called loudly.

Thigpen still didn't stir. A man walked through the doorway, surveyed the room, and scowled. He was tall and blonde, with a wide-brimmed hat and a shiny gold badge on the lapel of his jacket. He glared down at the prone body, still deep in drunken sleep, then crossed the room and kicked the foot of the bed hard enough to shake the wall.

"Thigpen!" he said, voice booming. "Get up."

Thigpen rolled over then, put a hand to his eyes to shield them from the glare of sunlight from the door.

"Wha...who are..."

The man kicked the bed again.

"I said, get up," the man repeated.

Thigpen sobered in an instant, scrambled up the bed and against the headboard, shaking his head to clear the cobwebs.

"What do you want? Get out of my room."

"Not likely, friend," the man said. "You're going to want to get up, unless you want to be shot in your bed and create a scandal."

Thigpen grew silent. He threw his legs over the side of the bed, and stood, nearly falling backward as the remnant of the night's alcohol hit him full strength. He was close enough to the wall to prevent a fall, but his voice was slurred, and his movements were sluggish.

"Who...are you?" he asked.

"It's funny that you don't know that," the man said. "Very funny, I think, since you've been flashing my badge around the tavern, claiming to be a man of the law, trying to rape local women—any of this getting through? Story ring a bell? I'm going to say this one time...you get yourself together. You strap on whatever iron you carry, and you get outside. I'll be waiting. I'm watching the door, and others are watching the window. I'm going to give you a chance you don't deserve. You meet me out front—one of us will walk away, the other will help fertilize the local crops. If you kill me, you'll have an honest chance to be gone from here before others show up to kill you or lock you away."

"You have the wrong man," Thigpen said thickly. "I am a duly appointed..."

"Five minutes," the man said. "Five minutes—outside, face me, or I shoot you like a dog."

The door was suddenly empty and Thigpen reeled, nearly collapsing back over the bed. He dropped and knelt there for a moment...then he rose. He stared at the door, and then, as if in a trance, he turned away. He crossed the room, buttoning his shirt, and tucking it back into his jeans. His gun belt hung over the chair where he'd left it, and he grabbed it, fumbling it around his waist.

Every step he took, every movement he made, his balance improved. His coordination returned. He recovered almost as if controlled by some unseen force. His lips curled down at the corners, and the ice-chip eyes chilled. Lenore saw this, saw the sudden transformation, and shivered. Then, as he headed for the door—the world shifted again.

Edgar wrote furiously. He had tossed aside his story in progress after only a few moments and begun anew. The words flowed so quickly through his thoughts that his fingers were cramped, and more than once he'd had to toss aside a pen and just grab another in fear of losing the thread.

It was like nothing he'd ever written before. He tried, just for a couple of moments, to pinpoint the inspiration. All of his writing came from twisted versions of things he'd seen, or done, or read. This was unfamiliar, raw and very powerful, and he had no idea why it had come to him.

Grimm had stepped closer, bending his head inquisitively toward the paper. The bird rarely showed any real interest in what he did, and this was another thing he wished he had the time to contemplate, but he knew the old magic when it wrapped around him, and he sensed nothing malign in whatever this was. Even if he had, he would not have pulled away. He trusted Grimm to drag him back to reality if he got in over his head, and he'd had just enough of the whiskey in his flask to unleash his own shadows. He could be dangerous himself, if provoked, though he preferred to direct that at the pages, impaling them with quills and staining them with the ink of his nightmares.

The story grew from the roots of a great tree. It stretched up into shadows. He frantically recorded his impressions, the moon's face glaring down through intricately bound branches. Eyes—dark, hollow eyes without life—stared back from the heights, and the mist from some hidden body of water rose like tendrils of cloud to slip in and out between those branches, leaves, and ghostly-images.

Beyond the tree, he saw an open stretch of ground. In that space, two men faced off. One was tall and blonde, beefy and intense. The other was dark. He blended into the chilly air and the wisps of mist. His eyes were cold, dead chips of ice, and though he stood at an odd, ungainly angle, there was a sense of speed and confidence in the set of his jaw, and the loose way his hand hovered over the butt of a holstered pistol.

Edgar knew the tales from the west. He knew the gunfighters, the lawmen, the wild savages and the mountains of gold. He'd met them and lived them in the words of others, in the newspapers and the stories of strange, dark men in taverns. It was how he built the fantasy worlds that bound his own stories. He plucked the details. He listened, and then he thought about what he had heard. He brought characters to life in his mind and then he let them flow back out through his fingers.

This was subtly different, and yet, very similar. The two men were not cowboys, but they faced off in classic, end-game stances, the angry challenger, and the calm, snake-quick killer. That much was obvious—the larger man, in some odd way, represented the light, and the dark man had a slimy, dark aura about him. He smiled, but it was superficial and fragile, like a porcelain mask painted carefully and placed over something hard and ugly. The first movement, a twitch of the lip, or the raising of an eyebrow, would shatter it.

Edgar wrote. He built a story around it—a long road, a chase, a string of bodies stretching down roads leading west. The road ended with a woman—a girl, really. Her fate hung in the balance.

Then something shifted. He felt a surge, and knew that the dark man would win. He would aim and drive a slug of lead through the better man's heart. He would take the girl, and disappear into the night. He would send the man's spirit drifting to the trees and the fog.

It was too much.

With a burst of will Edgar reclaimed the pen. The story fought him, flowing on toward its conclusion, but he concentrated, gritted his teeth painfully, and dragged the quill across the paper. He marred the ending. He slashed across the words and recreated the image. He feared he'd be unable to do it justice, that all the words and work would be wasted and it would be too weak to do any good. Still, he wrote.

He raised the quill, dipped it into the ink, drove it back at the paper and continued. The dark man's smile splintered into a thousand points of obsidian. His hand shot down and the barrel of his gun rose, and the other man, a hair's breadth too slow, retaliated. Edgar's gaze shifted ever so slightly. A black blur passed before his eyes and, a moment later, before the eyes of the dark man as well. Grimm, it had to be Grimm, but it could not be—not in the story—not in the image.

The stories never leaked into the real world, or vice versa. They were just stories. The images—the characters—they suffered—he always made them suffer—but they were bearing the pain so that he didn't have to. They were projections—shades of reality.

This was not. This was happening, and what he wrote—how fast he wrote it, and how well, mattered. He had no idea how he knew this, or why he believed it, but it was true. Grimm had not dragged him out of it; instead, the old bird had joined the battle, adding his own dark speed and darker vision to the flow of ink and shadow.

Edgar wrote the bird's trajectory into the story. He drove it, like a blindfold, across the dark man's eyes. He couldn't stop the strike, the whipcord fast reaction or the snap of the trigger, but the bullet whizzed past its target—within inches. It might have actually grazed the tip of the big man's ear. It was enough. The second gun barked, and the dark man was driven back. The slug caught him directly above the heart. He spun, and as he spun, another shot caught the spinning shoulder, driving him into a pin wheeling arc toward the loamy ground.

He spun, and he fell, and when his narrow, hooked nose struck the ground, it drove through the soft earth and planted. He lay, at an odd angle, twitching. Smoke curled, just for a second, from the end of the bigger man's pistol. He stood very still, brushed his hand back along the side of his face, where the bullet had skimmed so close it left a red, burning streak.

Edgar tried to finish the story, to give it a proper ending, and seal away the shadows, but as he worked, the images faded. He fought a losing battle with his mind for control of the words. He heard the loud flutter of wings. He saw the dead man's blood, seeping into the ground. He saw a woman's startled face, and a drawing, a tree, and then a stream of faces, one after the other, roaring directly at him and dissipating to smoke as they brushed his eyelashes.

And then—as suddenly as it all began—it was gone. He sat stunned, staring at the scratched, torn paper on the table and the ruined, brutalized tip of his pen. Grimm was nowhere to be seen, and from what seemed very far away, he heard a woman's cry, and the crash of something falling.

Edgar pushed back from the table, lurched to his feet and turned toward the door. He needed air, and he needed to know what the noise was—why it seemed to echo as much from his thoughts as from the night—who had cried out, and why. More than anything, he needed to know the ending to the story. It lay crippled and unfinished, stillborn on the table and he felt as if—if he did not finish it—he might never write again.

The air sizzled with power. He recognized it—knew it did not concentrate in such measure without provocation—but did not believe he was capable of such a burst on his own. He'd seen many strange things, recorded most of them in prose and verse, and set them aside, moving on as much as was possible. This experience had shaken him to his core, and he was not even certain that—when he opened the door—he'd find himself in the same world from which he'd entered.

He felt a breeze, and knew, somehow, that the window was open. He remembered closing it after Grimm's entrance, but he didn't turn. He grabbed the doorknob, jerked it open, and stepped out into the darkness.

As he moved into the chill night air, he saw that the door to his immediate right, the corner room, was also open. Lamplight streamed out and pooled on the wooden slats and the ground beyond. A woman stood there, silhouetted, staring into the distance. She turned, caught sight of him, and stared.

"Did you…" she said.

Edgar took in her eyes, her long hair, slender figure, and the serious set of her jaw. Something sparked between them, and he knew that she'd felt some—or all—of what he'd felt. Maybe caused it.

"No," he said. "I don't think so. Maybe a part…"

Another woman stepped out into the darkness behind the first. She was younger, darker, stumbling a little, and staring out beyond the porch through glazed, empty eyes. She paid no attention to her surroundings. Instead she stepped down to the ground and walked very slowly forward to where two trees stood about thirty feet apart. When she reached a point between them, she turned back.

"Here," she said. "It was here. They stood, there," she pointed toward the tree nearest to the bar, and then at the ground beneath her feet, "and here. Thigpen was shot here. He died. I was there."

"Thigpen?" Edgar said. He turned to the woman. "Who is Thigpen? The dark man? The one with the eyes of ice? The snake?"

Lenore nodded. She studied Edgar with new concentration.

"How do you know that?"

"I wrote it. I was working on a story—a story about a lost love. Something…interrupted me. I did not finish that story, but began another. Two men—a gunfight—a death. The darker man was going to win. I felt it, and I could not stand that it might be true, so I…changed it."

"Changed…?"

"There was no bird," Anita said softly. "I was here. He drew his pistol first. He fired first, but at the last second, he shied away. I thought it was the drink. I thought—maybe the sunlight was too much after so little sleep. There was no crow. I stood right where you stand now. There was no crow."

"I changed it." Edgar said. "He was evil. He was faster, and he was going to kill that man. There was a woman, as well…"

Edgar stared at Anita, concentrating.

"You?"

Anita turned to face Edgar, as if seeing him for the first time. She started to speak, stopped, and simply nodded.

"He is gone now," Lenore said.

"How long ago did he die?" Edgar asked. "What did I just write...see?"

"The gunfight happened a year ago," Lenore said. "His spirit was... detained. I was working to release it—and Anita was telling me his story. I'm afraid it's a little complicated—a little more so with your inclusion. I'm Eleanor MacReady. My friends—what few there are—call me Lenore."

"Edgar. Edgar Poe. I'm a writer, among other things. The boy from the tavern told me you keep odd hours."

Lenore laughed then, and the sound broke the heavy darkness that had wrapped around them. Anita still looked bewildered, but not frightened. Edgar leaned back against the frame of his door and stared at the trees. Now that he knew, he could see it. The entire encounter, as he'd envisioned it, played out once more in his mind. He saw where the men had faced off, where the one—Thigpen?—had fallen.

"I think we are going to have to discuss this, Mr. Poe," Lenore said, breaking his reverie. "If what you say is true, and you caused a change in the image that I shared with Anita—then you have reached into the past. Or, more curiously, you seem to have been a part of it all along. I find that more than a little odd. And there is the matter of the crow..."

At that moment, there was a rustle of feathers. Grimm dropped from the sky like a dark cloud, whirled up and under the overhanging lip of the porch, and thumped onto Edgar's shoulder, nearly knocking him from his feet. Anita screamed, and Lenore backed away, but Edgar stood his ground, regained his balance and reached up to steady the bird.

"It's okay," he said. "For better or worse, this is my traveling companion. His name is Grimm."

Anita stared, one hand to her mouth to stifle any further outcry.

"We need to get inside," Lenore said. "Come to my room for now. We need to get out of sight before anyone else comes out to see what's going on. I'm not sure I could explain why I'm talking to a stranger in the middle of the night, and I'm quite certain I have no explanation for—Grimm."

Edgar closed the door to his own room, and followed the two women inside. His gaze was immediately caught by the drawing on the table. He crossed the room and leaned down to stare at it.

It was a drawing of a tree, except, bits and pieces of it were missing.

There were five blanks in the branches, leaves, and gnarled bark—not places that seemed to have been left out of the picture, but bits and pieces that were simply…gone. One in particular held his attention. He reached down and traced it with the tip of his finger.

"That's where I found him," Lenore said. "That's where his face was trapped—his spirit. The tree held five spirits. It happens when someone fights very hard against moving on after death, or when some event—some tragedy or traumatic event—causes an unnatural binding."

"What bound him?"

"I don't know…at least, I'm not sure. Now I think…"

Lenore turned and stared at Grimm.

"He's not just a bird," she said.

"No, far from it," Edgar said. "I have told you he is my traveling companion, but it would be more accurate to say—I am his. He is very old, very intelligent, and I believe he is responsible for the visions that bring my stories—the insights that allow me to bring dark events to life with simple pen and ink."

"He is your familiar," Lenore said.

Edgar frowned. He knew the term well enough, but not the context. It was a word normally associated with witches, practitioners of dark arts. He thought he might have recognized it from his research, but had certainly never associated it with himself.

"Don't look so shocked," Lenore chuckled. "It's a very old term, and very apt. You, and the bird, are bonded. He is as bound to you as you are to him, and that is why—when you needed something you did not have—a way to change what had already happened—he became your vessel.

"I am not certain about this, because, as far as I know I'm the first practitioner of my own art, and nothing like this has ever happened before, but I believe that it's possible this man—Thigpen—was waiting for you. For us. He was trapped for a reason. I think, just possibly, Mr. Poe, that you have bent time. It's a very impressive feat, I must say."

Edgar stared at the picture.

"The others?"

"Free," Lenore said. "Normally I'd know at what point that occurred, but I have no memory of this room, or the work, since Anita's story drew me in. I assume it was about that time that you yourself were caught up—an unexpected blending of energy, but, if I am correct, perfectly in accordance with something bigger—something grander."

"Fate?"

"Perhaps."

Anita, who had stood silently off to one side, staring, slowly approached Edgar. Her gaze was fixed on Grimm, and she moved forward with tentative courage. She held out her hand, obviously expecting the old crow to snap at her, nip off the end of a finger, something. When her finger brushed the top of his head, Grimm dipped at the neck so she could scratch more easily. When she did so, and then pulled back, he set to work preening his feathers.

Lenore laughed again.

"He is the only one of us not caught up in the how or what of it."

"Probably for the best," Edgar said. "So...you think something or someone—obviously more powerful than you or I—saw the dark outcome of a gunfight over a year ago, and, what, altered reality so that something distracted this man Thigpen, then trapped his spirit to await the opportunity to make that thing distract him?"

"Something like that. You have a better explanation?"

"There was no crow," Anita said, cutting in. "I was there, and there was no crow, but tonight—when I saw it tonight—I knew that it was right. I knew that it must be the truth." She turned to Edgar. "You saved my life."

Edgar stared at her, then back at the drawing on the table, and finally back at Lenore.

"I'm going to try and get some sleep," he said. "I suggest that the two of you do so as well. We will be able to think more clearly by the light of day, and I believe that we both have stories to tell—important stories."

"Anita," Lenore said, "will you stay?"

She nodded.

"I will get more blankets from the tavern. I have a key, and sometimes I sleep in an empty room, when there is one. I haven't liked walking home alone since..."

Grimm let out a soft caw just then, silencing her. Then, in a rush, the girl crossed to Edgar, threw her arms around him, including Grimm as well in an impromptu hug. She left the room then and Edgar stood, staring after her. Grimm, rumpled, hopped from foot to foot and glared.

"Tomorrow, then," Lenore said. "And well met, Edgar Poe. I believe we are well met indeed."

When she closed the door after him, he stood a long time on the shadowed porch, staring out at the trees, and the darkness, before slipping inside, closing his window, and climbing into bed for a long, absolutely dreamless sleep.

# Chapter Four

Breakfast was a fairly sedate affair at the tavern. Even the most hardcore of drinkers would not wander in until noon or later, so those who were awake, and aware, and present, took advantage of the silence.

The kitchen was open. There was toasted bread in large slices, soaked in butter. There were eggs, and there was bacon. The boy, Tom, had returned with a basket in one hand and a large sack over one shoulder. He'd struggled gamely under the weight, and when Edgar stepped out of his room and spotted him, he hurried over to lend a hand.

"I've got it," Tom said.

"I'm sure you do," Edgar said, "but I am going to assume that you remembered to do me a certain favor, and with that in mind, it's the least I can do to carry the basket to the tavern for you."

Tom grinned.

"Got the corn right here in my pocket," he said. "Whole bag of it. I know it's the right stuff 'cause my ma spends half her day chasin' crows out of the bin where we keep it."

"Sounds perfect," Edgar said. "Let's get this food inside."

Lenore was already seated at the table to the rear of the tavern, beneath the great window. Instead of shadows, the surface of the table was bathed in morning sunlight. Anita bustled among the tables, polishing the surfaces, wiping down the chairs. The morning was far less forgiving than the dark of night; food, stains, and stray glassware had found its way to the far corners of the room, and now kept her occupied.

Edgar took it all in in an instant, and smiled. He crossed to the bar, laid the basket on top, and turned to Lenore.

"Do you mind if I join you?"

"I would be offended if you didn't. I trust you slept well?"

"I slept as if every ounce of energy and strength had been drained from me. There were no dreams, and all things considered, I will consider that a boon."

Lenore laughed, and Edgar took a seat beside her, but not too close. She was drawing, and he didn't want to bump her arm, or to spill something on the work in progress.

"What do you see?" he asked.

"Nothing," she said. "I am as drained as you are. For once, I'm just drawing. It's difficult, creating art—and then cutting out pieces of it— knowing that once the faces and spirits are gone, I'll have to fill back in the blanks. It's how I make my living, such as it is. I sell the drawings. I do portraits. I draw or paint people's homes. It's not a bad life, but it's not always very lucrative, either."

"It sounds very similar to the life of an author," Edgar said. "I am beginning to do a bit better, but it has been a long road, and there have been...problems."

"You live in a cloud," Lenore said. "I saw it last night, but there was too much else to concentrate on. It follows you—and defines you. What is it that has caused such pain?"

"There are many things, but the worst of them is the failing health of my wife. Despite all that I have been able to do for her, none seems able to help. She wastes slowly away...I fear that soon I will lose her."

"Life is a cycle," Lenore said. She turned back to her drawing.

Edgar glanced down at the paper. She had drawn a crow in flight, wings spread and eyes bright. It reminded him of Grimm, and, at the same time it did not. This was a wild creature, young and strong. Grimm was strong—but his strength was of a deeper kind, and he was—as the farmers were fond of saying—no spring chicken. Still, somehow, she had reached inside, and drawn out the spirit. There was no doubt that it was Grimm, and there was no doubt that she possessed an incredible talent.

"It's amazing," he said. "I think you captured him in a different time, or a different life, but it could be no other."

She shaded the feathers of one wing carefully.

"Time does not work like that," she said casually. "It's not a string with an end tied and another winding off into some unknown dimension. It is more like...a plane. Do you study mathematics, Edgar?"

"I have dabbled, but I don't see the connection."

"There is always a connection. Some believe that time is a direct path, beginning to end. Others claim that it is a circle, or a figure eight, winding in and back upon itself like the serpent Ouroboros. History may run in cycles, but time? Time is a static thing. What is happening now—and what happened in your grandfather's time? Both happen simultaneously."

"It's an interesting theory," Edgar said. "But I am not certain it's quite right."

"No?" she glanced up at him. "Then how would you explain the fact that your bird—at the direction of your pen just last night—disrupted a gunshot that occurred a full year ago? Or how the spirit of the man that shot killed could have waited, trapped in the branches of a tree, for you to come along and do it? Is he dead now? Was he dead a year ago? Will he ever really be simply dead, or will he be alive, and dead, for eternity?"

"Questions too heavy for early morning sunlight, and offered before a proper cup of coffee."

"Laugh if you will," Lenore said. "I have seen this more times than I can count—never like what happened last night—but there are things that just can't be explained in a linear fashion. If it was not true, I suspect you'd be very short of stories—or at the very least, that your stories would be much more mundane and ordinary. I believe, never having read one, that they must be spectacular. Dark, deep, drenched in mystery—and pain."

"The latter is certainly true," he said. "I have been told more than once that my stories lack hope. That people want to be dropped into the shadows, but only if there is a ladder, or a rope that will bring them back into the light. I write, and I tell my tales, but it seems that I am fresh out of ladders, and there are no ropes in sight…"

"And yet," she said, "you sensed the need last night, and you responded. You write about the shadows, but I think—maybe—you dream of other things—lighter, happier things."

"Let's just agree," he said, "that it is progress that I dreamed of nothing this past night."

Lenore's smile widened. With quick flicks of her wrist, she added sprinkles of shredded corn dropping from the crow's beak. Edgar watched the way the muscles rippled in her arms, the way her fingers played across the surface of the paper, brushing aside flecks of lead and smoothing the surface.

"So, why are you here?" Edgar asked. "I can't believe it was accident. I mean—I believe you are traveling, and paying your way with your art. You are very talented. This just doesn't seem like a very…art conscious location?"

"You'd be surprised who might want a drawing, a portrait, or a painting," she said. "This area is filled with old money—it's as old as the country, after all. Still, you read me correctly. I sought this place out. You might say I was drawn here."

There was a loud squawk, and Grimm dropped to the windowsill outside. The bird cocked its head, tilting to one side to stare in at the two seated beyond the glass pane, and at the drawing on the table.

Edgar grinned at the bird. Lenore glanced up, smiled, and then shot back away from the table as if she'd been smacked. She nearly toppled her chair over backward, and it was all that Edgar could do to prevent her smacking her head on the floor as she went over.

"What…" he said.

She shook her head, and then pulled away. She was on her feet in an instant, staring at the window. Grimm sat there, met her gaze for a long, silent moment, and then, with a great cry, leapt from the sill and back into the sky. Edgar stood, stunned, and everyone in the tavern had turned to gape.

"Are you okay?" Edgar said.

Lenore shook her head again, and then turned to him. "I'm not sure. I…I saw something that I did not expect to see—something I can't explain. I'm not even sure that I should tell you—I…"

Edgar took her by the arm and led her back to the table. She took her seat, and he helped her organize her pencils and the loose sheets of paper she'd scattered. Anita walked over, her pretty features twisted in a frown of concern.

"It's probably nothing," Lenore said. "I just saw…I think I…no, I did. I saw something in Grimm—or on her—or—I'm not sure how to explain it."

"Her?" Edgar said.

Lenore turned to him and nodded. "I'm nearly certain. I would not have had any idea before but…"

"But what?"

"I saw a face superimposed over the feathers of the chest. A very young girl. She stared right at me—and I believe she is trapped."

Edgar stared at her, and then down at the drawing on the table.

"What will you do?"

"I…I have no choice," she said. "I will draw what I have seen, and I will set her free."

Edgar sat very still for a moment, and then, he nodded. He knew that what she did was the right thing for those who were trapped, but he had traveled with the bird for a very long time. If what was to come removed the magic—if it ended, and Grimm flew off into the trees and the swamp to never return, he was not certain that he could stand it.

Lenore studied the emotion burning from his eyes, the effort he made to remain calm.

"If she is meant to be with you," Lenore said, "she will be. The girl is trapped, but the crow—Grimm—is a familiar. Your familiar. I do not believe she was a party to whatever happened, or that she could be happy carrying another soul trapped inside her, but neither do I believe anything will be lost."

"If you did, though, you would do this anyway," Edgar said.

"I would. If I did not, I would slowly go insane thinking about it—wondering what evil I might have become a part of."

"And I," Edgar said softly, "will be utterly, and absolutely alone, I'm afraid, if something goes wrong. It is a recurring theme in my work. They say that art mirrors life."

"I don't believe that," Lenore said. "It imitates, at best."

She reached for her drawing of Grimm, and the gum eraser that sat beside it. She worked quickly, and as she worked, she spoke.

"Why does this remind me of a story?" she said. "I don't remember any stories of crows as prisons…"

"There is one," Edgar said softly. "Not a crow…a raven. It was written by the Brothers Grimm—you know their work?"

"Some," Lenore said. She didn't look up from her drawing. "Tell me. What was it called?"

"It was called," Edgar said, "The Raven. I will tell it in my own words—I've read it recently, and I have a good memory."

"I love stories," Lenore said.

"As do I. I just can't seem to find one with a happy ending. The Raven, as you might expect, starts with a young girl. It goes like this…"

# The Raven

## A Revision with Apologies to the Brothers Grimm

In a long ago time, and a faraway place, there lived a queen. The queen had a very young daughter, too small to walk on her own. The child was precocious, and no matter what the queen said, nothing could prevail upon the girl to listen, or to be silent. The crying of the child maddened the queen, and she stormed about the castle in anger until she happened to glance out the window.

Ravens circled the castle, a great unkindness of ravens. They screeched and cried out, and it reminded the queen of her child. She flung open the window in frustration and turned to her daughter.

"I wish you were one of them," she said. "I wish you would become a raven and fly away, screeching as they do, and leave me to my peace. Then I would have some rest."

Now, the story says that at this point, the child was instantly transformed to a raven, and flew away. That is not exactly so. There was an old woman who worked in the service of the queen—her name was Estrella. Though she was named star, there was no light in her. She was conniving, and versed in potions and dark arts she kept to herself. She sometimes cared for the girl as a part of her duties, and that very day, when the Queen made her wish upon an unkindness of ravens, she whisked the princess off to safety.

Later that day, she slipped away with a bag of seed corn in a pouch tied about her waist. She found a clearing in the woods, scattered her corn, and set her trap. It did not take long to lure several ravens close enough, and, eventually, the perfect vessel set off her trap. She scuttled back to the castle with her prize in an ornate iron cage, avoiding its darting beak and using a heavy cloak to muffle its cries.

Estrella lived in an upper room of an all-but-abandoned tower at the rear of the castle. Her rooms were drafty—hot in the summer and bitterly cold in the winter, no matter how she built her fire. None of this bothered her, for she was a sorceress, and the simple threat of weather was of no consequence to her. She rarely slept, and when she did it was usually to snatch a few hours during the brightest light of day, when she was least powerful.

She placed the raven's cage on her mantel and went to the old sideboard, abandoned and decrepit, that served as her desk. She had few possessions, and most of them would have had her burned at the stake, or drowned, had anyone in the castle ever seen them. They did not, of course, because—as I have said—she lived in an abandoned wing of the castle, and because she had laid an intricate sequence of charms and illusions on the entrance, and on her chambers. What others would find, if they managed to stumble into the room, would be an empty chamber, dingy and windswept, and they would find themselves drawn inexplicably to the doors.

She found what she sought; a thin leather tome with intricate, arcane designs worked into the cover and flipped it open. A moment later she gave a sharp cry that might have been elation, or even dark laughter, but evoked no sense of mirth. She was not in the queen's service out of fealty. She had a plan, and like the solving of a dark puzzle the pieces were falling into her hands.

It was a simple spell. She needed something from the raven. She needed something from the girl. Neither was a problem, as she'd been collecting bits and pieces of her small charge for more than a year. Trimmed locks of hair. Scraps of cloth. A favorite toy, believed lost. The bird she had all of.

She worked through the night. She designed a small talisman, formed of bits of the girl's life. She added things that sparkle and things with odd scents. She formed it into a small, dangling bauble and attached it to a string, which she then dangled into the raven's cage. At first, it only glared. It backed away and cried its baleful cry. She persisted. The small ornament caught the light from her candle and glittered.

The bird attacked. It grabbed the bits and pieces of the princess in its strong beak, screeching and rending, and as it did so, fast as a serpent, the crone plucked a single feather from its tail. She left her captive in frustrated battle with her talisman, and went off in search of the princess.

The girl was playing behind her mother's throne. There were thick blankets spread, and one of the queen's chamber maids watched in trepidation as the child seemed to stalk the most valuable items within reach, one after another. Each time she was chastised, the tiny princess let out a wail, and would not be calmed. Just as Estrella entered the chamber the child let out a shriek of outrage and petulant anger. The maid watching her dropped to her knees and tried to calm the girl, but she would not be defeated so easily. She sought her mother's attention and the only way to achieve her goal—for better or worse—was to get past the defenses set by her keepers. She redoubled her cries, and tried to squirm free.

Estrella moved in quickly.

"I will take her," she said softly. "I will quiet her, and get her food. When she has calmed, I will bring her back to you."

The girl nodded quickly. A few moments more, and the queen was certain to rush in on them, threatening curses and punishment.

Estrella took the princess, who, despite her desire to be with her mother, was always curious around the old woman. She sensed something different, and there were always interesting things to see, taste, and smell when Estrella watched her. She grew silent, and allowed herself to be lifted and taken from the chamber without further protest. The chamber maid stood and scanned the room. The queen was nowhere to be seen. She knew that she should not hand off her charge without direction, but she feared the queen's frustrated rage more than her anger at being disobeyed in a smaller matter. Estrella often watched the girl, and she could claim an honest mistake in believing she had done the right thing. If all went perfectly, the princess would be returned before anyone noticed, and there might actually be a reward for keeping her silent.

Estrella wasted no time. She carried the princess through the halls of the castle quickly. She cast a glamour around the two of them so none would notice their passing. As she climbed the stairs to her room, she smiled. It was her first genuine smile in years—possibly decades. The princess stared up at her, wide-eyed. She did not cry out, and she did not struggle. She sensed something—interesting—to come, and she waited.

Estrella carried the child to her bed and laid her carefully among the ratty blankets and threadbare pillows. She stared up and cooed, reaching out her chubby fingers for whatever might be offered.

Estrella watched her for a moment. On the mantel, the raven still tore at the talisman. For the second time, the crone smiled. She pulled the feather from a pocket in her dark robes and held it out to the girl, tickling her fingers and teasing it over her cheeks. The princess giggled, then laughed, and then with sudden speed, she snatched the feather from Estrella's grasp. There was no hesitation. Like every other thing that went into the baby's grasp, she shoved the feather between her lips and bit down.

The room shimmered. Though she knew what to expect, the burst of power still startled Estrella. She stumbled back from her bed, even as the raven perched where the princess had been only moments before stretched its wings and stared at her. She met that glassy-eyed gaze, studied it, and thought that—just for a second—she caught a glimpse of confused terror.

Then, without hesitation, as if she had flown every day of her life, the princess launched from the bed, whirled in a tight arc around the room, and took to the sky. Estrella watched, just for a moment, and then opened the door of the cage and released the raven.

"Watch over her, dark one," she whispered. "One day someone will come for her. If she is not safe, I will come for you."

The bird squawked, staggered a moment after being imprisoned in the tiny cage, and then, with a quick angry shake of its wings that sent down and feathers in all direction, it dove for the window and disappeared. Estrella walked to the window and gazed upward. The ravens circled the tower in a dark stream, agitated, and suddenly augmented by one.

When they curled around the far edge of the castle, and out of sight, Estrella turned back to her chamber and began to quickly gather her things. She had her own ways in, and out of the castle. She knew that the chamber maid would believe she had stolen the child, but it was unlikely the girl would admit to letting someone take her charge—at first. By the time she did, they might not believe her at all. Probably the girl would be put to death for her trouble, but that was no concern of Estrella's.

When they finally searched the castle for the old woman—she was long gone. The rooms where she'd stayed seemed as though they had been deserted for years. They found nothing at all, in fact, to mark her passing, but a rickety old wrought iron bird cage, and a single raven's feather.

The queen never recovered. She ranted, and raged. The king, who had been away at war, returned to find his daughter missing, and the explanation of that disappearance—sketchy. He knew how his wife had felt about the child, how she'd raged about the crying, and the misbehaving—as if the girl was old enough to attend her and wait on her hand and foot, instead of a babe.

The kingdom fell into disarray, and there was no heir. Eventually, the king grew old and his health failed. The queen tried to assume control, but the king had a cousin, a dark man with darker ambitions. The queen was locked away in the same tower of the castle where Estrella had lived. They sent men in to clean it, and seal it against the winter, but she was watched around the clock, and never allowed beyond the confines of her rooms.

Lenore pulled the pencil away from the paper and turned. Edgar, who had allowed himself to be caught up in the story, sensed the change—and stopped speaking. He shook his head.

"Where did that story come from?" Lenore asked him.

He glanced down at her drawing without answering. The near perfect image of Grimm had changed. In the feathers of his—her—chest, the face of a young woman stared back at him. He knew that was not possible, that the eyes stared at whatever the angle they'd been drawn at required, but he couldn't shake the sensation.

He looked up.

"It's like when I write," he said. "I would not be able to write as I do, or the stories that I do, without the link. Grimm somehow connects to my thoughts, shares memories, brings me visions. It has never happened before without him—her?—being very close.

"The story I just told is not The Raven—not the one that the Brothers Grimm penned so long ago, in any case. It is a new darkness, a shift of the sort that so often separates reality from fictions. If the Brothers did not record the story exactly as it happened, or if they merely repeated what they had heard passed down from oral history, it might explain the flaws in the original story. And still…I feel as if there is more, something powerful that I'm missing."

"Flaws?"

"The story of the queen crying out to the ravens, and cursing her daughter is dark, born of the frustrated rage of a woman not ready for motherhood. The rest of their story—a young man meeting the grown princess and going on a magical quest, where he finally frees her using a wand that can open any door, a cloak of invisibility and a magic horse, don't fit. It is more like two completely different stories. As if one were obscured by time—or—possibly by something more powerful—or someone."

"Grimm is not a raven," Lenore said. "The story is about a raven, not a crow."

"You've said yourself that Grimm is more than a bird. If there is power behind those dark eyes, and if there is truly someone trapped inside, is it possible—perhaps—that she has obscured it? That she has made herself common in order to obscure her nature? That she has bonded with me—one who can share her thoughts—because she is also trapped."

"That is not all you," Lenore said. "You are thinking out loud, but the thoughts are not random. You must have felt some of this, sensed it as you wove the words…"

Edgar turned back to the drawing. The girl inside was no child. In some way, she had grown. She should have been long dead, and so her growing had been painfully slow. She had been denied her childhood, denied interaction with other young women, adults, young men—and yet—in trade—she had known Grimm. She had learned and evolved and somehow the two—bird and girl—had realized that it was time for her to be free. Either that, or whatever curse had bonded them in the first place was set to play out, and they were all in danger of being swept up in its darkness.

"Astounding," Edgar said. "You must finish this. You must remove her, remove Grimm, whatever it is that you do…she must be freed. I have no idea what will happen when you do that. This is not one of your spirits that will shift up through the clouds and away. I am afraid that the consequences may be far-reaching."

Anita had wandered over as Edgar told his tale. She'd listened, rapt, to his revision of the Grimm Brother's tale, and she'd heard the conversation that followed as she worked her way around the nearby tables, polishing surfaces that had long been clean.

She stepped forward. "What if it is not so simple?" she asked. "What if it is like last night? What if you do this, and it draws you in—back, forward—to some other place, some other time? And the old sorceress—Estrella? Where is she? What will happen if you undo what she created? She said one day someone will come for her—the princess. Are you that one?"

Edgar and Lenore turned in a single motion and stared at the girl. What she said made sense, and it should have occurred to both of them.

"There is danger in trusting the words of a fairy tale too literally," Edgar said. "This story has been filtered through my mind, and—apparently— that of the crow as well. Or raven—or familiar. Whatever Grimm is, she has a part in this. I don't know how much of this I might have just made up."

"She is out there," Anita said. She shivered. "I felt something when you told the tale, like a cold wind. I heard your voice, but it did not seem like your words. Not the way you would tell it—I mean. Forgive me. I hardly know you, and I have heard none of your stories, but—it is what I feel."

The room had begun to fill with other guests. Wagons had pulled up with supplies, and a carriage filled with young men headed to the capitol in Raleigh had spilled its charges into the tavern, ready for a meal and a drink on the way through. The relative privacy they had enjoyed nearer to sunup had dissolved into a busy crowd.

"Anita!" the bartender called. "I don't pay you to stand around and gossip."

"I have to go," she said. "I will meet you in your rooms when I can."

She turned to Edgar then, her face troubled. "I wish you luck," she said. "It is forward of me, but I feel that you can use it. Be careful."

Edgar nodded, and Anita hurried to the bar. Lenore gathered up her drawing, pencils, charcoal and erasers. She packed them carefully. From inside her bag she brought forth two sheets of what appeared to be onion-skin. She placed them over the front and back of the drawing and slid it carefully into the bag.

"Shall we?" she asked.

Edgar nodded. "There is no sense in putting it off. Somehow all the talk of sorcery and trapped spirits has not inspired me to finish this tale by candlelight."

"Out of character," Lenore said. She smiled.

They rose, and with a quick wave to Anita, who nodded and smiled thinly, they left the tavern and turned down the long porch toward their rooms.

# Chapter Five

The work was even slower than it had been the night before. There was only the one face trapped, but Lenore had never worked an image like this. For one thing, she'd drawn the portrait of the bird without seeing anything. She had already had to rework it once to superimpose the girl's features, and she'd seen them only for an instant—an instant that had burned dark lines into her mind.

The paper was raw from the constant erasing of the lines, and the risk of damaging the paper, or smearing the shading was constant, and distracting. She removed Grimm from the center of that image one feather at a time, softly working in the details of a young and very beautiful face. She had thought of asking Edgar to talk, to tell her another story, to tell her about his love, Virginia, and their life, anything to break the silence and create the atmosphere that aided her work, allowing her to free her mind from the mundane world and be lost in her vision.

Somehow it didn't seem right this time. A story had brought them to this point, and any attempt to tell the rest of the story might send them both veering off track. Though happy endings were clearly not Edgar's forte, he might attempt one, and she did not know what would happen if he consciously tried to change things at this late point. It would be better that they saved what simple skills and powers they possessed until events had played out as they had existed, or at least as they'd been written. As she thought this, she smiled.

Edgar did not watch her work. He stood at the window, gazing out at the trees, and the huge, deep expanse of The Great Dismal Swamp beyond. He studied the sky, and he kept his eyes open for anything that might shift or change. It wouldn't do for some innocent to wander up in the middle of whatever was to come. Even if no one was hurt, he and Lenore would be in danger. What they accepted as their lot in life, others would see as sorcery, black magic, and evil. They had no time to talk their way out of trouble. It was not a thing he usually had to worry about, as his visions mostly invaded his mind, and his stories were written late at night or in the wee hours of morning.

As Lenore approached the final lines of the drawing, ever-so-softly rubbing away the last of what covered the princess' face, a shadow broke over the trees. Edgar watched as Grimm, circling in a slowly narrowing spiral, worked her way down to the earth just beyond the window. It still didn't feel right thinking of the bird as a female, regardless of what Lenore had seen. He opened the window. The bird met his gaze and hopped back and forth from one foot to the other. He, or she, was clearly agitated, and made no move to enter.

Edgar left the window open and stepped back slightly, but he did not break eye contact with his old friend.

Lenore brushed the tip of her pencil across the paper a final time. Two lines joined, and suddenly, the entire image began to shimmer. Edgar stifled a cry. Beyond the window, in the grass beyond, Grimm stood as if transfixed. The creature's eyes were wide, and its wings thrown back. The hopping motion had stopped—all movement had ceased—and the light around it brightened like the heat of a searing brand, or the glowing tip of a bit of kindling in a fire.

Grimm cried out, and Lenore pulled back in the same instant. She nearly toppled her chair in the effort to distance herself from the table. Edgar heard her and moved to catch her, thinking very briefly that it was becoming a habit. He lifted her to her feet, and they stood together and watched as the bit of paper rose from the table. It hovered, glowing as if on fire, about eight inches above the surface.

Outside, Grimm rose as well. Not in flight, but slowly as if drawn by some odd force none of them could see. Edgar sent a silent wish that no one would walk out the back door of the tavern at that moment, or glance out one of the windows. Whatever was about to happen could not be stopped, and there was no way they could explain it if asked.

There was a blinding flash of light. Edgar staggered back, but held his balance. Lenore toppled into his arms, and he held her, supporting them both. There was no sound. It was as if the world had melted away in an instant, and they could only wait for it to pass. Edgar wrapped his hands around Lenore tightly, pulled her against him protectively, and cried out.

"Grimm!"

There was a distant, answering cry, and then the light faded…and died.

Slowly, still clutching one another tightly, the two made their way to the window and looked out.

It was then that someone knocked loudly on the door.

Lenore spun, startled. She could see nothing at first. The flash of light strobed and filled her vision. She nearly stumbled, then regained her balance and took a step forward. She didn't know what to do. She wanted desperately to turn back to the window—to know what had happened— but if someone was to burst in through the door they might not be able to explain what was happening.

The knock repeated, and with a worried glance over her shoulder, Lenore crossed the room and leaned against the frame.

"Who is it?" she asked.

"Tom, Ma'am."

Lenore thought fast. If she just said they were busy, the boy might get—and spread—the wrong idea. Edgar was a married man, and she still intended to stay and fulfill her original purpose. She didn't want to give the wrong impression.

"I will tell him to come and find you," she said. "He is telling a story, and I don't want to interrupt him."

"I think he's gonna need to hear this," Tom said. "With all due respect ma'am, and this won't make any sense but—could you tell him it's about his bird?"

That stopped her cold. The bird? What did the boy know about the bird? What had Edgar told him? And if the boy was here about the bird, and the bird was outside the back window, who else was involved? She took a deep breath, opened the door in a rush, and dragged Tom through, closing it behind him with a quick snap.

"Hey…" Tom said. He tried to pull away, but she held him tightly by the shoulder.

"Wait!" she said.

Tom must have caught something in her gaze because he fell silent, and he stopped struggling. When she sensed him calming, she released him and backed away. She turned to the window.

Anita stood back to one side. Her hand was pressed tightly to her lips, either in dismay, or to stifle a cry. Edgar stood at the window, very still. The sunlight shining in around him gave him the aspect of a silhouette. His stance gave away absolutely nothing.

Lenore moved forward very slowly. She stepped up behind him silently and glanced over his shoulder. In the grass, just outside the window, a small dark heap lay prone on the grass. It was very still, and though she knew that it must be Grimm, it did not look like a crow. It was smaller, and glossier.

"Is she…"

"He," Edgar said. He still didn't move, but he spoke softly.

"Grimm…is a he. He is not a crow, but a raven. It was a glamour, a safeguard we have tossed aside."

Tom had moved up beside them. When he saw the bird lying still in the grass, he didn't hesitate. He pushed the window open wider, and slipped through, nearly spilling everything from the tabletop. He was out before they could stop him, or call out, kneeling in the soft grass and cradling Grimm in gentle hands. He stared at the bird for a long moment, and then rose, very carefully, and carried him back to the window.

"He's alive," the boy said. "I don't know what to do—but he's alive."

Edgar reached out, and Tom laid Grimm gently in his hands. Edgar cradled his companion, stepped back, and Tom slid back over the window sill. Lenore reached up and closed the window, and with Anita's help, drew the curtains across it. There was no way to know who might have seen Tom, or what happened before he climbed out the window, but it was too late to worry about that. They gathered around Edgar, and he glanced up. He caught Lenore's gaze, his own a wash of pain.

"It is leaking from him," he said. "The power—the energy. I feel it slipping away, and though I can feel it, and share it, I cannot make it stop."

Then he seemed to wake, suddenly, and his eyes glittered.

"The drawing!" He cried. "You didn't finish the drawing. You set her free, she is gone, but there is a hole in the chest. A hole in the heart."

Lenore lurched for the table. She knew, even as he spoke, that he was right. She'd gotten so caught up in what was happening, in what might happen, that she'd forgotten her duty.

The drawing sat where she'd left it. She had to gather her pencils from the floor, and the chair, where Tom had accidentally knocked them climbing back into the room. She smoothed the drawing and focused. She did not have the time she would usually take to drop back into the trance-like state she had grown accustomed to. She pressed the tip of the pencil to the paper, and began to draw. The image was fresh in her mind, and she knew she would get no help with it.

Grimm had changed. She knew that she could not draw the raven; she had to recreate the crow. She had to drop back under the control of a broken glamour and bring back what she'd helped to shatter. She tried to relax, but her fingers gripped the pencil so tightly her knuckles whitened and she feared the shaft of the pencil would break, sending the tip skittering across the page. She controlled it.

No one in the room made a sound. Anita stood back, breathless. Edgar waited, the silent bird held in the open palms of his hand, as if offering a benediction. Tom just stared, wide-eyed, uncertain what he'd been drawn into but aware enough to play his part and do nothing to spoil the moment.

The world grew still. It is possible that it was simply the gravity of the moment and the depth of their concentration, joined in a single wish—a single work—but all four would swear to the end of their days that something closed around them, something that prevented the world from realizing something remarkable was happening, while at the same time helping them hold onto the spirit they fought for, the inexplicably intelligent and powerful spirit of a bird—a single small, dark bird.

Lenore worked quickly and with abandon. She spent no time staring at the page, or worrying at details. She knew them, or she did not, but it was a race against time, her gift against entropy and the slowly leaking energy she had to contain. The feathers returned. The glistening quality, darkening where strong, avian legs began, the shape of the woman's face, blanked from the center of the original image, disappeared. She thought about the morning. She though how happy she'd been, drawing the bird for the sheer joy of drawing, drawing it so she could show what she'd done to Edgar—possibly even to Grimm—who knew what the bird saw, or felt, or appreciated?

She remembered how the sun had wound through the trees and played across the window. She let the memory of the scent of hot coffee, bacon, and hot bread return to her. She heard voices, though no one around her spoke, and she drew. Her hand flew across the page, returning lines, shading, highlights and subtle background shading. As she worked she forgot, even, to breathe. There was not much to do. It was such a small yet complicated task, a one-shot succeed or fail moment in time.

It seemed to her that it took an age to complete the work. She threw the pencil over her shoulder to distance it from the page. She pushed away from the table and stood, staring down at what she'd recreated. The image of the bird and the girl stood, staring at her from the windowsill with beady, knowing eyes. Just for an instant she was certain she saw herself reflected in those dark, glossy surfaces.

And then it was gone. All of it. The energy drained from the room. The walls seemed to draw in on them, shrinking the space where they stood. The light returned to that of late morning. She looked around the room. The others blinked and stared, as if waking from a shared dream.

It took only seconds to re-focus on Edgar. She walked over slowly and raised her hands beneath his. He stared down at the bird he held intently. There was no emotion in that gaze, no animation at all. His concentration was intense. Moments later, Anita and Tom both stepped close as well, joining their hands beneath the still body. They held their thoughts and kept their voices silent.

And then, with a shudder that nearly stopped their hearts, the bird grew stiff, stretched its wings, and very suddenly opened its eyes. They stared, and Grimm stared back. Then, with a shift so quick they could barely follow the motion the raven stood in the center of Edgar's palm. It turned so that it met each of their gazes in turn, then spun slowly and glanced up at Edgar. Without warning, or ceremony, it let out a raucous cry and shook, sending a cloud of feathers and fluff into the air to float around them like a cloud.

Edgar's expression, so taut and unreadable seconds before, melted to a bright, delighted smile.

"Is he…" Lenore asked.

She knew Edgar would understand what she meant. It was one thing that the bird lived, but the question remained whether or not the two of them would retain their connection. None of them understood that bond—not really. Even Edgar, who was a part of it, had stumbled into it. Only the bird seemed unperturbed. It squawked again and hopped from Edgar's hand to perch on his shoulder, turning to face the room. Then, without warning, and very clearly, the bird bowed.

Edgar laughed.

"I could not have put it more eloquently, old friend," he said. "It's going to take some getting used to, this new look of yours, but I think it suits you."

Grimm ruffled his wings and began preening. Edgar turned to Lenore.

"Thank you. I don't know what I would have done…"

"There is no need for thanks," she said. "I can no more turn from the tasks appointed to me, I think, than you."

"I don't mean to speak out of turn," Anita said, "but—the girl? The princess, if that is who was trapped—where did she go?"

"Princess?" Tom said. "Beggin' your pardon, Mr. Poe, but I sure would like to know what's going on here, and what kind of trouble I've gotten into. I'll already be late getting back to the tavern, but…"

Edgar turned to him.

"Why did you come?" he asked. "I mean, if you didn't know that Grimm was in trouble, but you came about 'my bird,' what drew you here?"

"He saved me," Tom said. "I mean, the bigger bird, the other…"

"It is one and the same," Edgar said. "I don't believe you have time now for the entire story, but possibly soon. What do you mean he saved you?"

"There was snake. I had gone out back of the tavern to dump my morning sweepings. I wasn't watching where I was going. We have a pile of wood, and just past that is where we dump the trash. Once a week, I bring the mule and the wagon and carry it off.

"Most days I watch pretty careful around there, being so close to the water and all, but today I wasn't payin' attention. One more step, and I'd have stepped on that thing—water moccasin as big around as a rake handle. It reared up to go for me, and there was a flash—faster than I would have believed possible. That crow grabbed the snake, lifted it up and dropped it back in the trees. Scared the soul out of me."

They all turned to Grimm, but the bird paid no attention to them. It was lost in a fit of grooming, and apparently unconcerned with praise.

"I just came to thank you," Tom said. He fidgeted from one foot to the other, and it was hard to tell if he spoke to Edgar, or to the bird.

"Grimm is a brave and loyal friend," Edgar said solemnly. "He must have taken to you. Possibly it was the corn. In any case, I must ask you a favor, for me, for the ladies, and for Grimm—for that is his name. I don't believe you've been properly introduced. I must ask that you say absolutely nothing of what you've seen and heard here to anyone. You may talk freely to those of us who are present, when you are in private, but no one must know that strange things happened here. They would not understand, and it could go badly for us all."

Tom nodded. "You can count on me sir. I'd best be going. They'll already wonder where I got off to. If you don't mind, though, I'd sure like to hear the story of the princess, if there really is one."

Edgar leaned forward and rumpled the boy's hair.

"You can count on it," he said. "Anyone who knows me will tell you that there is nothing I like better than to share a good story."

Tom shook his head, and ran for the door. He was out and gone seconds later, and they heard the heavy pounding of his feet as he tore up the porch toward the tavern.

"I will be missed, as well," Anita said. "I told them I was going to take my lunch and go for a walk."

"I am willing to bet," Lenore said softly, "you have traveled farther than you intended, even if it was just a story for idle ears. Run on. You can return tonight if you want. We may all have more to talk about—assuming the story has yet to reach its end."

"I sense that it has not," Edgar said. "I believe rest is in order. I could do with a nap, and I am sensing my friend here feels the same. I have no idea how to proceed from this point, but I am now convinced that the proper path will stretch itself out before us. Despite my intentions of coming here to finish up some writing, and yours—whatever they originally entailed—we have been anything but in control of our fates since meeting."

Lenore glanced at her drawing kit, and the drawing of Grimm and at the scattered utensils that had fallen from the table. She nodded.

"You are right, of course." she said. "But you must take this."

She carefully lifted the portrait of the crow from the table. She wrapped it deftly around two fingers and rolled with her thumbs until the portrait was a tube. She reached into her open drawing kit and produced a bit of ribbon, which she wound around the paper and tied in a quick bow. She held it out.

Edgar hesitated, and then took it with a nod.

"Perhaps it is safer this way," he said. "There is power in your art, and no way to truly know how much of it remains in the lines of this image. I will cherish it."

Grimm let out a soft caw and, once again, bowed.

Edgar turned and studied him a moment, then shook his head.

"New roads await," he said. "Another reminder for the weary of heart."

Lenore laughed.

"Will you dine with me this evening?" she said. "I'd like to tell you a story. I want you to know why I'm here, and what it is I hope to do. It's been a long time since I had anyone I could confide in without being considered a witch or a crazy woman."

"I'd be delighted," Edgar said. Then, with a quick flourish, he matched Grimm's bow, nearly unseating the bird in the process. "Until this evening."

A moment later, he was gone. Lenore stared at the closed door, and turned her head at a quizzical angle for just a moment, as if trying to figure something out. Then she turned and gathered up her things, packing them carefully away. Whatever might come of the evening, she'd not be drawing again this day.

When her room was straightened she lay back across her bed and put her arm over her eyes to block the late afternoon sun trickling in around the curtains.

As she drifted off to sleep, Anita's words returned to her.

"The princess—if that's who was trapped—where did she go?"

Darkness found her before any answers, and she dropped into a deep, dreamless sleep.

# Chapter Six

Edgar woke to the sound of men shouting. He sat up quickly and tried to orient himself. The sun had nearly disappeared from the sky, tipping the trees beyond his window in deep gold, but supplying little light. The voices sounded again, and he heard a commotion out in back of the building. He rose quickly, straightened his clothing and hair as best he could, and turned toward the door. Then he stopped.

A quick search located Grimm on top of one end of the curtain rod.

"Are you well enough to fly, old friend?" Edgar said. "I could leave you here."

Grimm landed on the table with a thump and glanced at the window.

"No, the door," Edgar said. "Something is going on in back, you might be seen."

With a soft squawk, the raven leapt into the air and glided across the room to land on Edgar's shoulder. Edgar smiled, opened the door, and stepped cautiously out onto the long porch. He glanced both ways, but there was no one in sight. Grimm took off with a loud flap of his wings and soared out over the trees. Edgar watched him go, then turned to Lenore's door.

He reached to knock, but before his knuckles struck the wood the door swung inward and Lenore appeared. Her eyes were wide, and she stepped quickly out beside him.

"What is it?" she said.

"Not sure. There is something going on down by the docks out back. I think we have to find out what it is. I don't know why, but I have the sense that it might have something to do with us. If there is any danger, we should know up front what we are dealing with."

"And if someone needs help…" Lenore said.

"Yes, we'll be there to do what we can."

They turned and hurried toward the tavern. The doors were open, and a small pool of light had leaked out onto the porch, but there was no one in sight. All of the sounds they heard came from the back of the building. Edgar stepped through the doorway first, and Lenore followed. They stared inside at an almost empty room. The doors in back also stood open wide.

There were lanterns lit along the walkway leading down to the docks, and the two stepped through the main room and out the far side. It was about fifty yards from the back of the tavern to the water. Boats arrived at all hours of the day and night, dropping and receiving passengers and supplies, but any sort of normal traffic on the waterway wouldn't cause such a ruckus. If there was serious violence or gunplay involved, those inside would have hunkered behind their tables or slipped off to their rooms, hoping to avoid being shot. The place was absolutely empty. Not even the bartender, or a serving girl had been left behind to watch the till.

Edgar turned, looked at Lenore, and raised an eyebrow.

They started down the path toward the water.

"Get her up here," a voice cried. "I have a blanket."

The sound of water splashing and loud cursing followed. As they drew near, they saw men and a few women circled, holding lanterns. There was a raft tied up at the dock, but there were no boats in sight. Some of those on shore were pointing at something in the water.

"Damn it!" a man cried. "She bit me!"

There was a sudden flurry of splashing. Men bellowed, and those on the dock worked frantically to light the struggle, but whatever was happening in the water was moving too fast.

"Get more lights," Someone called. "Someone get a boat!"

"Use the raft."

"It's too hard to maneuver...get a damn boat!"

The cries flew back and forth in rapid succession. Edgar worked his way down toward the bank, keeping well back from those involved. He scanned the faces of the onlookers. Their eyes were wide, and they scanned the dark water intently, each hoping to spot something the others had missed.

"What happened?" Edgar asked a man in a dark suit.

"Not sure," the stranger said. "Something about a girl in the water. Giving them quite a run for it, it seems. Someone said she had no clothes."

Lenore studied the trees on the far side. Beyond those trees The Great

Dismal Swamp stretched out into the night. It seemed endless, and very suddenly, she sensed that immensity, and how it pressed in on their tiny, dimly lit stronghold.

Then a very different sound intruded. There was a sharp whizzing, followed by the sound of something being struck. A man cried out. The sound repeated, and suddenly everyone in the water was less interested in being there. Men dove for the shore, or the cover of the small dock. Those on the shore backed away, uncertain. Then an arrow shot out of the night and stuck in a tree about four feet from where Edgar stood with a solid WHAP! The crowd broke and ran, all but Edgar, and Lenore, who stepped back behind two of the larger trees near the shore and waited.

Edgar edged around the tree, angling to get a look at the far bank of the waterway. There was no one clearly visible, but as he watched he saw a face, surrounded by wisps of gray hair, press forward through the trees. A moment later, two large men, and a slender girl crept onto the beach. They stood very still for a long moment, waiting. When there was no reaction from the tavern side, they hurried to the water.

They entered without hesitation, and moments later climbed back onto the shore. Between them they supported another young woman. Her hair was long, hanging in damp strings down her back to her waist. She wore nothing at all, and moonlight gleamed off the pale curves of her body. As the two men half dragged, half-carried her into the trees, the girl who'd accompanied them kept her back to them. She held a long, supple bow, and an arrow was notched. A quiver rested easily on her shoulder, and Edgar saw the feathered ends of several more arrows waiting to be fired. He chose not to become their target.

"Did you see?" he hissed.

Lenore nodded, but even as she did, there was a solid THUNK! as another arrow embedded itself in the tree directly behind Edgar's head. He fell silent, and they waited. After several moments of silence, Edgar once again chanced a look around the trunk of the tree. There was no one in sight. The shoreline was bare on both sides of the water, and there was no sign that anyone had passed.

He stepped around the tree, and inspected the arrow. It was very long, thin and solid. Though obviously hand-made, he could find no fault in the workmanship. It was beautifully fletched with what appeared to be the feathers of a red tailed hawk. Where it bit into the tree, he saw a wickedly sharp metal barb.

"Glad I was on the other side," he said.

Lenore stepped up beside him and studied the arrow, then glanced back at the trees nervously.

"I'm sure they're gone," Edgar said.

Lenore shivered. She didn't look fully convinced.

"What just happened?" she asked. "I mean, who was that girl, and who were those—others? Some of the men who were out here had guns, why did they take off running the second that first arrow flew?"

Edgar didn't answer. He had turned, staring at the water, as if lost in thought, or trying to remember something. Then his eyes widened.

"Damn!" he said. He started for the dock at a run. Lenore followed, though more slowly.

"Where are you going?" she cried. "Why...?"

A moment later, his purpose became clear. He laid down on the dock and peered over the edge. A moment later, he reached down and pulled. A man's prone form bobbed under the edge of the short pier and then floated. Edgar held the man by his collar and dragged him toward shore. Another of the arrows protruded from his shoulder, and he was not struggling.

"Is he...?"

"He's alive," Edgar said. "Get up to the tavern and bring help. He's too big for me to carry, and I don't want to do any more damage. See if there's a doctor."

Lenore took off at a run, and Edgar continued, slowly, to drag the unmoving man toward the shore.

The man, Jebediah Nixon, was breathing raggedly, but he was unconscious. The arrow wound, while deep, was also clean. It had struck true, and run straight through, the tip protruding from the back of his shoulder. By some miracle, it had missed damaging anything of vital importance. The wound had bled a lot, and he was in shock, but a traveling veterinarian who'd been staying on the Virginia side of the roadhouse had cleaned the wound, doused it with enough whiskey to make Jebediah bellow, and stitched it up neatly. The scar would not be pretty, but the wound would heal.

As it turned out, Jebediah had served in the war under General Lee, and it wasn't his first battle wound. Once the burning from the whiskey had passed, and the ache from the wound settled to a dull throb, he was easily pacified by more whiskey poured slowly into a tumbler.

Everyone had gathered back in the tavern. Enough ale and whiskey had been poured to calm nerves and loosen tongues. After helping with the injured man, and accepting a round on the house, Edgar, his soaked sleeves and shirt drying slowly, and Lenore had retired to her usual table to wait and see where it would all lead.

"Who were they?" Edgar asked no one in particular. "I've seen Indians, and those two larger men were no Indians. Still the girl was incredibly accurate with the bow and arrow."

"Did you see the old woman?" Lenore asked.

Edgar nodded. "Only for an instant. She appeared first, just before the girl."

They stared at one another for a moment, and then, suddenly Lenore burst out laughing.

Edgar cocked an eyebrow and waited.

"We sound crazy," she said, fighting for breath. "The two men who were not Indians, an old woman who disappeared, and a girl with a bow and arrow, stealing a naked woman from the shore and disappearing into the swamp. If you were to write this into one of your tales, how do you suppose your editor would react?"

"I've not had all that much luck with editors thus far," Edgar said, "but I get your point. It is crazy, and it didn't start with the girl in the water."

Anita stopped by their table. She'd been kept busy serving drinks and taking orders for more. It was the first chance she'd had to stand still.

"They are not Indians," she said. "That was Nettie. The men serve her—the girl—no one is sure. Nettie has always lived in the swamp. When my family came to the swamp, she was already here, and she seems—the same. There is always the old woman, and the young girl."

"What are you saying?" Edgar asked. "She's a witch?"

"There are things in the swamp," Anita said, "that I do not understand. When the harvest comes, there is a celebration. Nettie is a part of that—or the girl is—or both. No one ever quite remembers."

"But the woman in the water," Lenore said. "Where would they take her? Where do they live; why did they shoot that man with an arrow?"

"No one knows where she lives," Anita said, "and no one will follow her in there. Some have tried. Most of them never made it out of the swamp alive, and those that did found no trace. If she took someone into the swamp, we won't know why unless she tells us."

"You talk to her?" Edgar said.

"Many have talked to her. She can heal, and they say she has the power to help find lost things, or to change your fortune. There is always a price."

Lenore shivered.

Edgar turned to stare out the window into the swamp. He had heard two words that drove into him like a steel blade. Heal—and change. One of the reasons he was on the road was to consult with specialists over Virginia's health. The answer was always the same. Some claimed to have cures, or procedures that would help, but they sounded like madmen, and as desperate as he was, he would trust none of them near his wife. This felt different. There was a lot of power in this swamp, and near it. Strange things had happened since the moment he'd arrived, and none of them appeared to be coincidence. He had approached Virginia with such solutions in the past, but she had rejected them. Her faith was strong, but apparently not strong enough to stop the withering of her health.

"I believe I could find her," he said. "Or, more precisely, I know that Grimm could find her. I don't know what would happen if I did, but I feel—somehow—as if it's something I have to do."

"What in the world are you talking about?" Lenore asked. "You know nothing of the swamp, and it appears to me that if you manage to get too close, what's likely to happen is you'll be shot. You are a handsome man, Edgar, but you will be much less so with an arrow protruding from your heart."

"You are forgetting about the girl," he said. "You freed her, Grimm carried her. I won't abandon her to some crazy woman in the swamp without at least trying to save her."

"What if she doesn't need saving?" Lenore said. "What if this Nettie knows what has happened, and knows what to do, and all you manage is to interfere?"

"You'd really be content not knowing? This is not as simple as one of my stories, or one of your drawings. There are powers stretching out through time. There are tales within tales, and powers within powers. It's like walking the roads of a dream within a dream. I can't just let it go. It's begun, and that's how it is with stories. There is a beginning, conflict, and an ending. I'm afraid I'd go mad without knowing all three."

As Edgar talked, the boy, Tom, had worked his way closer across the room. He pretended to sweep the floor, but he'd been eavesdropping, and he already knew more than most.

"I can guide you," he said.

He stood, red faced, expecting to be silenced, or sent on his way. Instead, Edgar turned and regarded him seriously.

"You've been in there?" he asked.

"I fish in there, and I've hunted with my pa, and my uncle," Tom said. "I can take you in, and I know the old stories. I know where to take you—

where she might show up. If you find her…that's probably as far as I go."

Edgar nodded. "I will need to see something from your father, and from the tavern keeper, showing that you are allowed," Edgar said. "You may tell them that we are going hunting, which is true. If I find Nettie, you are released with full pay."

Tom could barely contain his excitement.

"I believe," Edgar said, "that you'd better get back to your work, if you want a favorable decision from the bar keep. He's watching you, and he is not smiling."

Tom turned and hurried away, swiping the broom randomly at the floorboards.

"You really mean to do this?" Lenore asked.

"I do. I had hoped that you…"

"I cannot," she said. "I would, if I was free to, but I have my own quest—my own nightmares and demons to exorcise. I did not come here randomly, as you guessed. Before you leave, I will tell you—but at that point, I'm afraid, we must part ways, at least for a time."

Edgar smiled, but there was little humor in it.

"It seems I am always parting from someone," he said. "But this one time, I will allow myself the hope that when our tasks are complete, our paths will cross again. It would give me hope, and that is something I am too often without."

Lenore smiled.

"Let's finish these drinks, split up, and see if we can get any more information," she said. "I think we've had about enough adventure for one day."

Edgar nodded.

At the table next to theirs, the veterinarian who'd patched up the unfortunate Mr. Nixon sat with a large mug of ale. He'd pulled away from the others, and seemed lost in thought.

Edgar walked over.

"Good for that man you were here," he said. "He might easily have bled out from a simple wound without proper care."

The doctor looked up, momentarily confused as he was pulled from his thoughts.

"Oh, thank you," he said softly. "I'm certain someone would have helped him. There are military men here, and more than a few of them have encountered injuries much more serious without a doctor's aide."

"Still," Edgar said, sliding into the chair opposite the man, "I believe he was lucky, if there is such a thing. My name is Edgar, Edgar Poe."

"Simons—Brentley Simons. It was a brave thing you did, pulling him out of the water as you did. How did you know they would not come back and turn you into a human pincushion as well?"

"Honestly?" Edgar said. "I did not know. I merely acted, and I am sure, had I not done so, that another would have acted in my stead. I almost didn't chance it. All I could think of, after the arrows stopped flying, was that everyone had run back to the tavern and forgotten he was there. I heard him cry out when he was hit."

Simons nodded. "The thing I cannot fathom," he said, "is why. I was here at this very table when it all started. A man came in from the docks, very excited. He'd seen a woman, floating in the water. She was naked, and he didn't know what to do. That—I believe—is the crux of the matter. If he'd simply pulled her out when he found her, none of the rest of it would have happened at all, and we might have some answers instead of a mystery."

"The locals seem to know something of our bow-hunting strangers," Edgar said. "When they realized who was out there, they disappeared like smoke."

"I wondered about that. It was a tense, dangerous moment, but their reaction seemed out of proportion. I followed along, but I believe, if they'd stayed, I'd have done that too. I was caught up in the crowd."

They fell silent for a moment, sipping their drinks. Then Simons spoke again.

"You know," he said, "that was an odd wound. I mean, I'm not used to treating men, and I've only removed arrows from dogs, and one cow. Hunter claimed he thought it was a deer—owner claimed the hunter was drunk. I think maybe it was a bit of both. The thing is, I did study anatomy, and I read the journals. I guess what I'm saying is that, in a pinch, I wouldn't be a bad man to have around in an emergency."

"I believe we could get Mr. Nixon to vouch for you," Edgar said.

Simons chuckled.

"The point is," he said, "while Mr. Nixon is a lucky man, it had little if anything to do with me, and everything to do with how, and where the arrow struck. Nearly a miracle, I'd say."

"Why?"

"Did you get a good look at the arrow? The tip was hand made from jagged bits of metal. Looked as if it had been pounded into shape, and then honed like a razor. It's a wicked piece of work, and not designed to wound. In fact, half an inch higher, and it would have severed his Axillary artery. There is no way you could have gotten him ashore in time, had that happened. He'd have bled to death in moments. A little more to the side, and there could have been irreparable damage to the bones and muscle of the shoulder. If we were in a city, they might have saved full use of the arm, but out here?"

Simons shrugged and took a long drag from his beer.

"What I'm saying is, that shot was either a miracle, or absolutely perfect. It caused him to release the woman, who, by the way, gave him a nasty bite on his forearm for his troubles, but it did not cause any permanent damage."

"You don't think it's a miracle?"

"Did you get a good look at Mr. Nixon, Edgar? I'm not much of a church-goer, but from what I know of miracles, they are generally reserved for God-fearing folk. Unless I'm missing something, I'm going with perfect shot. Whoever that was out there in the woods, they didn't come here to kill anyone."

"Then what?"

Simons shrugged.

"I guess we'll never know the answer to that. As far as I can tell, no women have gone missing around here. No carriages have arrived since the one that brought you. She could have swum here from somewhere on the Virginia side, or been dumped off a passing boat. Without knowing who that woman is, it's a matter of simple mathematics. We don't have enough variables to solve for why."

"A mystery, then," Edgar said. "I'm no stranger to those. Unfortunately, I am used to creating them in my head, and writing them down. I'm afraid my real-world detective skills are untested."

"A pity," Simons said, "But I'm not sure what there is to learn here. Whoever those people were, and whoever that woman was, they're gone now. That's some of the wildest land in this great country."

He turned to the window and waved toward the swamp. "The Great Dismal Swamp is not named idly, Mr. Poe. Those who know it well are few and far between. It's not a good place for a casual stroll, or even a well-planned expedition by those who don't belong. If the bears, wolves, or snakes don't kill you, those with secrets worth dying for most surely will. If I were you, I'd get back to your pretty lady friend, and enjoy the rest of your stay. With a bit of luck, the excitement has passed."

"I suppose you're right," Edgar said. He drained his glass.

"In any case, I don't think anything else will be happening tonight. Enjoy your beer, doctor, and perhaps our paths will cross again."

"At the very least, over breakfast," Simons said.

He rose, and they shook hands, and then, with a quick nod, Edgar returned to where Lenore had resumed her seat.

"That was interesting," he said.

She raised an eyebrow. "You first."

"The good doctor—his name, by the way, is Simons, informs me that the shot that did not kill Mr. Nixon, or maim him, was either a miracle, or miraculously accurate. He leans away from divine intervention."

"That's the impression I got from the bartender," she said. "He knows of this old woman, and her 'minions'—as he calls them. She's been out there in the swamp as long as he remembers, and he claims to have heard tales about her from his father, and even his grandfather. The way he tells it, she's not a killer—but everyone here is afraid of her. Dark powers. Dark rituals. Deals with the devil. You name it, someone around here believes it of her."

"So, they won't be sending out a search party, then," Edgar said.

"Not likely. A year from now, they'll still be telling the story, embellished and turned into something fanciful, but the only time lawmen show up here is to try and keep the body count down. They don't cross the waterway into the swamp without a very good reason, and apparently an unknown naked woman being hauled off by a swamp witch is not considered that important."

"I must admit," Edgar said, "that I find this less strange than most would, and more intriguing. My own road often edges up against the shadows, and I've seen some strange things. Grimm has shown me others. This would barely register, except…"

"I know," Lenore said. "The woman. It's too strange to be a coincidence. And the others…if we're right—if what I think we are both imagining is true—how did they know? How did they make their way to that shoreline at exactly the right moment to carry her off? What do they know?"

"That," Edgar said, "is what I intend to find out. I don't have many days before I must turn toward home, but I will spend them, I believe, climbing through the swamp like a fool with a young boy and an old bird for a guide."

"It's like you said before," Lenore said. Her voice was soft, and her eyes were open wide, as if seeing something he could not. "It's like walking through a dream, within a dream. What if you don't come back?"

"You will have to find me, trapped in the branches of one of the old, dark trees," he said. "You will draw me, a handsome likeness, I would hope, and you will set me free."

Very suddenly, both their eyes filled with tears. Edgar rose and turned away.

"I have to go," he said. "I have to find Grimm, and I have to rest, and prepare myself."

Lenore reached out and laid a hand on his arm. He placed his own over it.

"If I don't go now, we may both miss our destinies," he said.

She pulled her hand free.

"Be well, Edgar," she said. "I hope that you find her—and I hope you solve your mystery. If you find Nettie—I hope she can help you save Virginia."

"You never told me your quest," he said.

"I'm tracking a dream," she said. "I had a vision—a woman trapped in this swamp, near the waterway. Her spirit is bound in a tree, not like the spirits I usually free, but something more powerful—more lasting. It's as if she's calling out to me."

Edgar stood very still.

"A woman," he said. "Trapped. I am beginning to feel as if we are not the gifted, or the cursed. What we are is pieces in some grand game—a dark game, with no good endings. This woman—do you know who trapped her—or why?"

Lenore shook her head. "I know that she has been there for a very long time. I could almost draw what I saw from memory, but there are tiny details that are elusive. I might capture them—or I might not. One thing I have learned is that I never get a second chance. Once I have drawn a thing, and then changed it, the link is broken. I have the talent to recreate the art, but not the magic—if that's what it is."

"So you are going to try and find the tree," he said.

"I won't have to try very hard," she said. "When I asked about it, I learned that there is a local legend. In the swamp, there is a large lake— Lake Drummond. On the shore of that lake, there is an old willow tree. The willow tree is so much in the shape of a woman that there have been legends about it since before white men came to the Carolinas. When I told them I'd like to draw her, I was given a map."

"You need a guide," Edgar said.

"I know. I will find one. I was hoping that Anita might know where the tree is located, or that she knows someone who will take me. It's not the same kind of dangerous journey you are planning. The tree, and the lake, are visited regularly by hunters and fishermen. There are trails."

"Bears can use trails," Edgar said. "It's only marginally safer."

"Bears don't use bows and arrows," she said. Then she smiled.

"I'll make you a bargain. You go on your search, and I will go on mine. I suspect I will be finished first. Whichever of us returns to this place before the other will wait. Before you return to your wife, and your work, and before I move on to whatever comes next, we will share stories one last time. And a drink."

Edgar smiled.

"I would like that very much. You have a bargain, lady. I will find you here among the lost souls, trapped women, and birds. I find that my own state has improved, if only slightly. Where I was once likely to travel in the presence of a murder of crows, I find I will only be burdened by an unkindness of ravens. It gives me heart."

Lenore rose then, and embraced him quickly, then, before it could turn to anything more, or the moment be broken irrevocably, Edgar stepped back and turned for the door. As he walked out into the night, he did not look back.

Moments later, glancing at the bartender to be certain he wasn't seen, Tom rushed out after him. Lenore watched the empty doorway for a long time. She was nearly certain, when the two were out of sight, that she heard the flutter of dark wings on the night wind. She tried to smile, but it was cut short as a shiver suddenly transited her spine.

# Chapter Seven

Tom caught up with Edgar before he reached the doors to his room. Edgar heard the footsteps, and turned.

"I'm gonna need some things from home," Tom said. "If we're going into the swamp, we can't just walk in empty handed."

"Will you be ready tomorrow?" Edgar asked.

Tom nodded. "Sure. I just have to tell Mr. Barnes—the bartender. I got a cousin Will who can come in and take my place for a couple days. You got any older clothes? A gun? A pack? We may be in there overnight."

"I'm afraid I only came prepared for a road trip," Edgar said.

"You and my pa, you're about the same size," Tom said. "If you was to send him some money…"

Edgar chuckled. "If you think your father won't mind equipping me properly, I would be grateful," he said. "I have no desire to perish of foolishness, and I have the feeling wandering into a place as wild as this unprepared would be exactly that. Would ten dollars suffice?"

Tom's eyes widened. "He'd sell you a set of clothes for that," the boy grinned. "You leave it to me. I'll be back here at by dawn."

"You can make it a little later, if you don't mind," Edgar said. "It's been a long day, and I suspect I'm going to need extra rest."

"I have to be back anyway," Tom said. "I'll have to show Will what to do. Should I bring more corn?"

Wings beat powerfully above them, and a dark speck dropped from the sky, spreading its wings and slowing to land on the ground a few feet away with a heavy thump.

Edgar turned and studied the raven. If it had been a robin, or a goldfinch, he knew that he'd recognize his old companion. He did not know how, but he was grateful for the knowing, and for the bird's presence.

"What say you, Grimm?" he asked. "More corn, or will you hunt The Great Dismal Swamp?"

The bird waddled over to them, lifting one foot at a time in an awkward shuffle. He turned his head first to Edgar, and then to Tom, then, with a quick squawk, pecked suddenly at the ground, kicking up dust.

"Corn it is," Edgar said.

"It's really him, isn't it?" Tom said. His eyes were wide. "I mean, the crow."

"None other," Edgar said.

Tom glanced up at him.

"You're not like anyone around here," he said. "We farm, fish, and hunt. We know secrets, and usually keep them. My pa told me about the old witch in the swamp, and about how important the festivals are—how they keep the land fertile—help us grow.

"But it's different. We live here by the swamp, and there are a lot of strange things in there—old things we don't understand. I don't know how to say it—not bein' good with words—but you seem to walk in a different world. I'm just tryin' to say, thank you for taking me along. Thank you for trusting me. If you'd not paid me a nickel, but asked me to go—I'd've done it. I just wouldn't be able to come here every day, sweep the floors, and see those trees out back without wondering what I'd missed."

Edgar ruffled the boy's hair.

"I hope you are still of such a positive mind about it when all is said and done," he said. "I have no idea what we will find out there. Grimm knows, or at least, I believe he does, but our link is tenuous at best. We share visions from time to time. If I need him, he always seems to be there. I'm not sure that I have ever really returned the favor."

"He was there for me, too," Tom said. "With that snake."

"So he was. Either you have a bit of the connection yourself, or you have a part to play in all of this—something he knows, that we do not. We are bound to the earth by fate, and by gravity, so we will have to plod along and follow what clues are available. I suspect, since we've been drawn into all of this without any concern for whether we wanted to be—there is no reason to believe we'll be able to get out of whatever has hold of us until it's over."

"You think we're…meant to find her?" Tom said. "Like…"

"Destiny." Edgar said. "Exactly like that, I'm afraid. In for a penny…"

"In for a pound," Tom said.

He frowned, shook his head, and when he looked back up at Edgar, he was grinning.

"That works for me, Mr. Poe. I'll see you in the morning."

"Until then. And Tom?"

"Yes sir?"

"Call me Edgar. I think we're well past the Mr. Poe stage."

Tom nodded, turned, and hurried back toward the bar. Edgar opened the door to his room and stood aside. Grimm hopped up and glided through the entrance. Edgar followed, closing and locking it behind him.

Lenore left the tavern shortly after Edgar. As it turned out, when she'd asked the bartender, Barnes, about the tree, the man had actually suggested that Anita show her the way. The girl was familiar with the area, and he'd noticed that the two of them had hit it off.

"A lot of strange things have been happening around her," Barnes said. Most of them started when you came in drawing those pictures. The rest seem to follow your friend, Mr. Poe. I know Jebediah is grateful for the saving of his life—and that counts for something—but I'm thinking the sooner you finish your work and make your way out of here, the sooner we'll get back to the normal run of things. Duels, thieves slipping across the border, old Virginia men trying to marry their young cousins. You know—normal problems."

Lenore didn't know if he was joking, serious, or uncertain, but she took him up on the offer of Anita's company.

"I made a promise," she said. "I promised that, when I was done, I'd wait, if Mr. Poe doesn't return before I do. I'll make another...the minute that promise is kept, I'll move on, and leave you to your...normal life."

Barnes went back to polishing his bar.

"I'll hold you to that."

Lenore took her leave then, and returned to her room. She thought that—maybe—she might try to draw again—just for herself—before she slept. Instead of a bird, though, the image that troubled her was very human. Dark hair, darker eyes, and pale skin. And the words. Without any other gift at all they would be enough to make him magic.

# Chapter Eight

Despite his warnings to Tom to not come around too early, Edgar woke with the dawn. He had slept long and well, and felt refreshed, despite the adventures of the day before. He'd expected to toss and turn, ending up writing late into the night, but he hadn't even glanced at his quills, or his ink. He'd poured himself two fingers from his flask, readied himself for bed, and brought out his worn copy of Grimm's Fairy Tales. He didn't know what had possessed him to do it, but he'd finished his drink and worked his way through several of the old stories.

They were dark. Every one of them. He knew they'd been written for children, but he couldn't imagine sending a young soul to bed with the images they provided. Others who felt the same had already begun revising the tales, retelling them in watered down versions that hamstrung the storytellers' bite, but allowed the children who heard them to sleep at night without bright lights or screams. He wondered briefly if that was how it always was with magic. It started out vital and potent, and then, over time, as men and women fought to possess it, hide it, steal it, and decipher it, it grew more and more obscure.

The fairy tales were like his own stories, he realized, but his made no pretense of being fairy tales for the naïve, they were a way of exorcising the heavy loneliness of his existence, the frustration of being unable to help his wife, and the dimly glowing, low-burning lamp that was his career. The problems that his protagonists faced, the agony he put them through, served to boost his own spirits, at least to the level of mild melancholy. He knew he should be grateful. He made his living doing what he enjoyed, more or less. He had gifts that others did not share, or even suspect. He had Grimm, and Virginia loved him. Those two things alone should have tipped the balance in his favor and lifted his spirits.

Nothing seemed able to do it. Nothing fully broke through the shadows—only the words gave him even partial respite. When he wrote—and sometimes, if the story was good enough—when he read the words of others, the perpetual weight on his heart lessened. The fairy tales he'd read had lightened his spirits in the same way the dismal, hopeless fates of his protagonists did. In a certain perspective, it improved his state. Things—as they said—could always be worse.

As he waited for Tom, he organized his papers, and found himself agonizing over what to take, and what to leave behind. He couldn't rid himself of the idea that he was embarking on more than a simple walk in the woods, and that—if not impossible—returning to this place, this room, and whatever he left behind would require more of him than any task he'd ever faced. He would not be able to solve this by writing it into a story.

Somewhere in that swamp, there was a woman. That woman had been traveling with him most of the days of his adult life—trapped inside a companion he felt he needed to discover anew—and now she was alone. Alone, of course, was a relative term in this case. The old woman in the swamp had known the girl was coming, and had spirited her away, but to what end? In the story—The Raven—the Brothers Grimm had attributed the transformation to a sorceress. That sorceress had not lived in a swamp, or even in the Americas. In fact, as was true of most fairy tales, it was written without any degree on detail, or time. What good would it do to read a story meant to frighten, or teach a lesson, if the child knew that it took place hundreds of miles from their home, and a century before they were born?

There was a knock on the door, and he laid aside his book to open it. Tom staggered in and dropped a large bundle on the floor at Edgar's feet.

"Good morning," Edgar said, staring down at the pile.

"Good morning, Mr. Poe," Tom said. "I think I brought everything we need. I would have brought less, but when my ma and pa found out we were going into the swamp, and why, well, they threw in a few extras. I wish they'd have let me bring the mule, but they need him to pull the cart, and there'd have been no one here to lead him home."

Edgar squatted and poked through the bundle on the floor. He pulled out a pair of coveralls, clean, but very worn. There were boots, and he noted that, though they were not something he would wear into the office back in Pennsylvania, they rose to mid-calf and appeared to be in decent repair.

"Those're Pa's spare work boots," Tom said. "There's snakes in the swamp, and a lot of mud. You wouldn't make it a mile in what you've got. Same with your clothes. No offense, Mr. Poe, but you aren't really equipped for any kind of hiking at all."

"None taken," Edgar said, "and I told you—call me Edgar. I'm grateful to you, and to your family."

He lifted the boots out and found an old canvas pack beneath.

"What's this?"

"I got my own bag," Tom said, turning to show the pack slung over his shoulder. "You'll have to help with some of the food and water, a few other supplies. I figured you might want some of your own things too. That pack should do you good for most everything you've got. We can fill that flask at the tavern, if you like."

Edgar smiled. He hefted the pack and turned it over in his hands. On the flap, tooled into the leather, was the name Zach.

"Who's Zach?" Edgar said. "Won't he be needing this?

Tom glanced at the floor and lowered his voice.

"Zach—he was my dad's brother. He fought with the infantry when the states split up. He was killed, tryin' to get a friend of his off a battlefield. They found his pack, and they brought it home to Pa. No one has used it since, and we figured—well—I told them about Jebediah Nixon. They figure—a hero's pack…"

"I'm no hero," Edgar said. He studied the pack more carefully. "I will treasure this, and we will get it back to your father in one piece. It's almost like you read my mind. I was going through my things, trying to figure a way to travel in the swamp with my bag."

Tom grinned. "I'm going down to the tavern. I have to show Will the ropes, and I'll see about getting the supplies we're going to need, what I didn't bring at least. We should be ready to go in about half an hour."

"I'll change, and get packed, then," Edgar said.

"There's a flannel shirt there, too," Tom said. "It's pretty warm by day, but at night, it can get darned cool. I have our bedrolls out front. Wasn't able to get a tent but I got a tarp, and I know how to rig it, if we need it. We should be able to spend the night in the shack I know—a place Nettie might come."

"I'm glad you're coming along, Tom," Edgar said. "I'd be lost out there."

Grimm chose that moment to float down from the top of the doorframe, circle the room, and land directly atop the pile of clothing on the floor. He glanced up at Edgar, and let out a soft squawk.

Tom glanced down at the bird, shook his head, and smiled.

"I think you were already in pretty good hands," he said. "Thing is, a bird would have had a heck of a time totin' these bags, and I'm not sure he can pitch a tent. I reckon I'll earn my money."

He turned and left the room, and Edgar carried the bundle of clothing and supplies to his bed. He stripped and changed into what Tom had brought him. The overalls were a little loose. His slender frame didn't carry a lot of muscle. The boots were snug and a near perfect fit, and the shirt—while it smelled of burned tobacco and lye soap, was a good fit as well. He snugged his belt around the center of the overalls and turned to the pack. He tucked in his books, his paper, quills and ink, and left the flask on the table. He really did want to refill it—he had the feeling it was going to come in handy.

There was rope, a knife, a bundle of dried meat, and a few other items already in the bag. The last item he stowed made him smile. It was a small bag of corn, carefully bundled and tied with a bit of string. He turned to Grimm and shook it at the bird.

"The boy is grateful," old friend, "as am I. At least one of us will eat well on this journey."

Grimm paced in a circle, then hopped up and glided to the table. He eyed the flask, as if watching his reflection in the polished metal, and then settled back to wait. Outside the window, the sun had risen higher, leaking through the uppermost branches of the trees.

"A good day for an adventure," he said to no one in particular.

He opened the door, and Grimm hopped to the sill, and then out, beating his wings mightily and soaring up and over the trees toward the swamp.

"I will see you on the trail," Edgar said.

There was no answer. Grimm wheeled up and over the trees, and was gone.

Edgar felt a little bit ridiculous stepping into the tavern, dressed in his borrowed clothing, with the pack slung over his shoulder, but no one paid much attention. In truth, he looked less out of place than when he wore his own clothing, blending in with the lumbermen and travelers. Tom was waiting near the bar. He had several small bundles at his feet, and he was deep in conversation with the bartender, Barnes.

Edgar scanned the room but there was no sign of either Lenore, or Anita. He didn't know if he was relieved, or disappointed. He decided on the former and stepped up to the bar.

"Good morning, Mr. Poe," Barnes said. "I understand you are trusting this young ruffian to lead you off into the swamp."

Edgar smiled.

"He's a good boy, and he tells me he knows the way."

"If anyone here knows, it's him," Barnes said. "If you are really searching for Nettie, though, no amount of savvy will do the trick. You're going to need an edge."

Edgar cocked his head to the side quizzically.

"Whiskey," Tom said. "You've got your flask, but that's for you. You'll want a small bottle for her. That's what the old 'uns say, anyway. You want her help, you go to the old hunting shack, and you bring her something to drink."

Edgar thought about it. His research was far from the ordinary run of facts, politics, and biographical trivia. There were a great number of stories about witches, spirits, forest magic, and most of them involved one form or another of offering. Here, on the edge of civilization, bordering one of the largest and greatest wild spots left, an offering of whiskey seemed oddly appropriate. He wondered if he'd be asked to sprinkle it on the Earth, or set it aflame in some arcane pattern.

"We certainly don't want to go in unprepared," he said at last. He pulled his flask from the pocket of the coveralls and placed it on the bar. "Fill this, and we'll take a bottle of whatever you feel is appropriate. I'll wrap it in my pack to keep it safe."

Barnes reached beneath the bar and pulled out a small, sealed and stoppered bottle of dubiously colored liquid.

"Corn whiskey," he said. "It's cheaper, and she won't mind. Anything else would cost you more than double. We only get shipments monthly—I can't afford to sell much of the good stock by the bottle."

Edgar nodded. He wrapped the package carefully in a spare pair of socks and tucked it deep into the center of the pack.

"It's sealed good," Barnes said. "Unless you crack it on a rock or something, it will be fine in there. You find Nettie, you tell her I gave it to you. That's on the house. Never spoke with her myself, but I've seen her a time or two. You never know what you might need, though, or who you might want for a friend."

"I will do that," Edgar said. "And when I return, I promise that I will bring a story. I can't promise it will be a happy story, because mine seldom are, but I can promise it will make you think, and that—if I learn anything of your swamp that you do not already know—you'll find it in the words."

"You are a strange man, Mr. Poe."

"So I've been told," Edgar said. "I'd rather be strange than boring. It's a flaw in my character."

Barnes chuckled.

"Have a good trip, Mr. Poe. I'll see you in a few days, God and Nettie willing. I'll buy you a drink."

Edgar nodded, pocketed his flask, and handed the man his payment. He turned and found that Tom had already moved to the back door and was standing rather impatiently, bobbing from one foot to the other. Edgar smiled, because the motion reminded him so much of Grimm.

"Let's get going then," Edgar said. "Lead the way."

Tom turned, and Edgar followed him out the back of the tavern and down the path toward the dock. He knew they had to cross, but was uncertain how it would be accomplished. He hoped they wouldn't have to wade—starting the journey wet to the skin did not appeal to him.

They reached the dock, and Tom clambered down onto the raft without hesitation. Edgar regarded it dubiously, and then followed.

"If we take it to the other side," he said, "how will it be returned? They won't need it until we come back?"

Tom laughed.

"It's like a bridge," he said. "There's a rope tied to it. When we're on the other side, we'll pull it up on the bank. In a little while, Mr. Barnes will send someone down to pull it back before the rope can get caught up on a passing boat."

The simplicity of it struck Edgar, and he laughed.

"It really is a good thing you're here," Edgar said. "I probably would have waded across."

"You'd have to swim." Tom said. "The waterway is very deep. It has to be so that the bigger sailboats can pass through to the locks up in Virginia. With that pack, you'd have drowned.'

They stared at one another for a moment, and then Edgar burst out laughing again.

"Just get us to the other side. We have to get on with this journey so I can find some point at which I can reassert that I am the adult. So far, I'd have died more than once without you—either from the cold, the lack of shoes, or drowning—and I haven't even set foot in the swamp. I'm beginning to feel as if I'm in a bit over my head."

"Maybe," Tom said, not laughing, "that's why your bird saved me? He sure seems to look out for you."

"That he does," Edgar said. "That he does. And now you have joined him. I'm a fortunate man."

Tom turned, untied them from the dock and pushed off, launching them across the nearly still water toward the far bank. Edgar couldn't help scanning the trees and remembering the arrows, and the large figures who'd flanked the old woman during her brief appearance.

The crossing took only a moment. On the far side, Tom leaped from the boat to the bank and hauled on the rope. Once the corner of the raft had lodged on the bank, Edgar followed, and when they stood side by side on dry ground, he helped to draw the small craft far enough up the bank that it wouldn't slide away in the current.

"They'll come for it shortly," Tom said.

Edgar nodded. He stared across the water back at the dock on the far side and the tavern beyond, as if locking the image in his memory. Then he turned and stared into the trees. He felt as if he'd stepped straight out of one world and into another. Standing on the ground and looking up the length of them, the pine trees felt taller than they'd seemed from the dock. When he finally lowered his gaze, he saw that there were several trails leading off into the swamp. He studied them carefully.

"Which way?" he asked. "And where do they all go? Who has reason to journey into the swamp?"

"There are folks who live back there," Tom said. "Some trap, some hunt and fish, but others—they just don't want to be found. The trail on the left leads back to where there are some cabins, and even an old church. The right trail leads back to the lake. It's a good long hike, fairly clean. We need to take the center trail. It goes straight back in, just to the left of the lake. Mostly hunters use it—some fishermen, but only those who are really serious. It's the trail you'd take if you were going in and not planning on coming out—if you take my meaning. It's the way to the shack we're heading for where most folks say Nettie can be found, if she wants to be."

"If that is supposed to make me feel better," Edgar said, "it has fallen short. I certainly hope that we'll be coming back."

Tom grinned.

"Don't you worry Mr. Poe," he said. "I'll get you there and back again, wherever there turns out to be. If we're looking for Nettie, we only have to go in so far. The shack I mentioned is about two miles in. It's a kind of jumping-off place. From there, a lot of different trails go on in deeper, some toward the lake. There's usually firewood, and if you use it you're expected to replace it before you go. If you sit outside with that bottle, my Pa says Nettie will find you."

"If that doesn't work," Edgar said, "at least we'll have a roof over our heads the first night."

Tom grinned.

He turned, hefted his pack onto his back, and headed off down the middle path. Edgar followed. After only a short while, the trees rising up on either side, and the heavy, moist air wrapped around them, enhancing the impression Edgar had of walking into the pathways of some other, older world. Edgar studied the plants as they passed, memorized the trees, their leaves, the flowers that lined the trail. He wanted to remember. He didn't know why, for certain, but he needed to know that it would stick with him—that he'd be able to recall it—possibly to write it down. He wanted to be able to paint the images with his words as clearly as they came to him.

They worked their way in deeper, and the light from the sun dimmed. It trickled down through the leaves and foliage. It dappled the ground with white disks of light that danced with the breeze. There were bird calls, and all around them the sounds of animals told him they were not alone. It was wild, like the country must have been when only the Indians roamed the land. Edgar felt it. The swamp was a very old place, and powerful.

One thing was becoming clearer with every step he took. A mile in the swamp was not the same as a mile on the road. The trail was very rough, not traveled often, and at times barely recognizable. Tom moved forward with confidence, pointing out areas where the footing was uncertain, ditches filled with undergrowth and leaves that might catch an unwary ankle, and at least once a coiled snake sunning itself in what light was available, not a foot from the trail. Once or twice they stopped and waited as the boy listened to rustling in the undergrowth, or strange guttural sounds emanating from the shadows.

The boy kept up a steady rain of chatter that tapped at the edges of Edgar's thoughts without penetrating too deeply. He spoke of family, spread around the state and as far west as the Mississippi. He talked about farming, hunting, fishing, the trees they passed and the animals whose sign he found. Edgar nodded at the proper moments, and shook himself free of his thoughts now and then to ask a question, or point something out, but for the most part his thoughts were far away.

He should have been leaving for home. Virginia waited, and as ill as she was, he did not like losing any time with her—dark as it might be. He half-wished he'd not come on this fool's errand at all, but knew at the same time there was no choice involved. The minute he'd become aware of Grimm's strange cargo—it had fallen on him to find the end of the tale. If he could just have written it, he would have, but Lenore had changed that.

She brought a new dimension to the images. Before he'd had dreams, and shared pain with the denizens of shadowy half-realities. Once converted to words and pressed onto paper, they diminished, releasing him. This was different. This time he'd seen the girl's face. He knew that in some way it all related back to the Brothers Grimm, or at least so closely alike to what they'd written that there could be no doubt of a connection. It made him wish for a few moments to discuss the story with those esteemed siblings.

The connection meant that the story that had been started, and the true ending, had never been joined, and he found himself locked in the center of it all, moving toward that truth without care, toward what might happen when he arrived. It was usually not his lot to live the basis for his stories, but only to experience the melancholy and pain. That was another thing that seemed different. For once, he was unconvinced of a bleak outcome. In The Raven, there was a happy ending. In this version, that ending was skewed, and yet, if he stretched the reality of it enough, the original story might be more of a map—or a key—even a prediction. The young man who fell in love with the princess did not meet her while she was yet a raven, but while she was trapped in an inaccessible prison.

And even while trapped, the princess was able to get out long enough to give her lover all the information he needed to free her. First, she sent him into temptation and bid him resist. In typical human fashion, he did not, and so, she sent him on a quest.

In the end, there were three keys, and Edgar could not help but believe that they were still in some way relevant. A staff—possibly a wand?—that allowed one to open doors. A cloak or some method of becoming invisible to the naked eye, and a magic steed that could cross any land or terrain to reach its objective. Very powerful objects indeed, and for the most part unlikely to exist, but as so many other things in life, these might be but symbols with much simpler, or complex explanations.

He wished he had time to sit and think it through. There might be any number of meanings behind the stick, and in the story to win the horse that enabled the hero to reach his love, he had to use his wits to best three brigands who were quarreling among themselves. It had all the signs of a truly grand puzzle, and the makings of a story unto itself.

The sun had risen directly overhead, and there was more light than there had been. Herons and Cranes abounded, fish jumped in nearby pools and streams, and more than once Edgar was stopped cold by the sound of branches breaking, or some other noise he could not immediately account for. None of it fazed Tom, who continued on down the barely discernible trail as if he were out for a Sunday stroll. The deeper in they went, the more completely cut off they became from anything familiar or normal.

"This," Edgar said, stepping around the log of a rotted tree that had fallen across the trail, "must be what it was like for the first Europeans to visit here. If I didn't know we'd left scant hours ago from a well-lit tavern, I might convince myself this wilderness stretched forever."

"If you keep going the way we're headed," Tom said, "it might seem that way. The swamp is a big place, and Pa says—for the most part—the interior is unexplored. Things change in here, water shifts, patches of land that you remember from earlier trips are either in a different spot, or plumb gone. There's been men from down Old Mill way walked off into the swamp and was never heard from again. I even heard a fellow say he'd seen a thing in here, like a man, but hairy. I saw an ape in a circus once—sort of like that, he said, but tall like a man. I wouldn't' want to meet it, whatever it was.

"There's a lake near here, Lake Drummond, where I don't go unless I have to. Lots of folks fish there, and now and then someone hires a guide just to go in and see the trees. There's a cypress there looks so much like a deer folks say that's exactly what it is. They claim hunters were chasing it, and it couldn't escape, so it changed itself into a tree and could never find its way back."

Edgar wondered briefly if Lenore would see that tree, and if so, if she would try to set the animal free as she'd done for so many others. He thought the answer was yes, and he had a sudden yearning to see that drawing…and her face.

To clear his thoughts, he said.

"I don't know a lot about your swamp, but I've heard of Lake Drummond. There's another legend associated with it that even a man living as far from here as I do would be familiar with it. They say there's the ghost of an Indian maiden, a girl who died just before she was to be wed, who haunts that place. I have a friend back home, a poet—and a minstrel, of sorts. His name is Thomas, like your own, Thomas Moore. He wrote about that girl, and her lover. I've heard him sing it.

Edgar then began to sing softly. His voice was not a great one, but he could carry a tune, and the memory of the song carried him back to other places, and other times.

## The Lake of the Dismal Swamp

"They made her a grave too cold and damp
For a soul so warm and true;

And she's gone to the Lake of the Dismal Swamp,
Where all night long, by a firefly lamp,
She paddles her white canoe.

And her firefly lamp I soon shall see,
And her paddle I soon shall hear;
Long and moving our life shall be
And I'll hide the maid in a cypress tree,
When the footstep of death is near."

Away to the Dismal Swamp he speeds—
His path was rugged and sore,
Through tangled juniper, beds of reeds,
Through many a fen where the serpent feeds,
And man never trod before.

And when on the earth he sank to sleep,
If slumber his eyelids knew,
He lay where the deadly vine doth weep
Its venomous tear, and nightly steep
The flesh with blistering dew!

And near him the she-wolf stirr'd the brake,
And the copper-snake breathed in his ear,
Till he starting cried, from his dream awake,
"Oh when shall I see the dusky Lake,
And the white canoe of my dear?"

He saw the Lake, and a meteor bright
Quick over its surface play'd—
"Welcome," he said, "my dear one's light!"
And the dim shore echo'd for many a night
The name of the death-cold maid.

Till he hollow'd a boat of the birchen bark,
Which carried him off from the shore;
Far, far he follow'd the meteor spark,
The wind was high and the clouds were dark,
And the boat return'd no more.

But oft, from the Indian hunter's camp,
This lover and maid so true
Are seen at the hour of midnight damp
To cross the Lake by a firefly lamp,
And paddle their white canoe!

"Pretty," Tom said. "I've heard the story, but never the song. Heck, I didn't think folks up north really thought about us much down here. Like you, they travel through, sometimes they stay long enough to fish, or hunt, or gather some stories to tell while drinking around their fire. Lake Drummond—she's a big one, dark, deep, and filled with secrets. So my Pa says. There's trees there that look like soldiers, animals, men and women. Nearly every one of them has a story attached if you dig far enough and ask among the old ones.

"Come harvest time, they have a festival down by Old Mill. There's a tree they pulled out of the swamp and turned it into a sort of pole. At the top, the branches are twisted like the antlers on a stag. At the festival, there's a feast. After the food's been served, they send us young'uns home. I don't know what happens on the night of Harvest Festival, but I know there's a fire, a big one, and I've heard my ma say it's the only time ol' Nettie comes out of the swamp. Not sure I even want to know what it's about, though I know I will. This year I'm old enough. Might even be chosen Harvest Lord."

"Sounds like a great honor," Edgar said gravely. Secretly, he wondered if he should worry for the boy. He was familiar with similar ceremonies around the world, but had not really been aware they still took place in America. In many, the Harvest Lord became a sacrifice.

"Pa was Harvest Lord when he was my age," Tom said. "He never talks about it much. I've tried to get him to tell me what happened, but every time I ask he gets this look in his eye. I just let it go."

Edgar breathed an inner sigh of relief and smiled. The events of the last few days were getting to him, and he was seeing dark magic in everything around him.

They broke through the trees then, and the low, shake-shingled roof of a cabin came into sight. Wisps of mist rolled around the base of a short raised porch. The windows were dark and shuttered. Nothing moved anywhere nearby. As they crossed the last clearing and started up to the porch, Edgar realized that he was exhausted. He wasn't used to this sort of activity, and though it had only been "a couple of miles" he felt as if he'd been walking all day.

He scanned the trees, and, as if waiting for them to notice, Grimm circled down out of the upper branches and landed on the porch rail. The old bird cocked its head to one side and watched them with what appeared to be either complete boredom, or deep concentration. Edgar let out a short laugh and lowered his pack to the wood floor of the porch.

"It's good to see you too, old friend," he said. "We'll get settled here, and then, I suppose I will get my pens, and my paper, and a candle, and sit here on this porch pouring dreams onto paper until this Nettie either appears or does not."

"I'll set up our bedrolls," Tom said. "I can get a fire going and fix something to eat."

Edgar stretched and nodded. "That, my young friend, is the best offer I've had in a year. I have to start getting out more. I should not be this tired."

Tom disappeared inside, and Edgar stood, staring out into the swamp, listening to the birds, and insects and all the odd sounds so alien to his life and his world.

"We have passed the veil," he said. Grimm hopped to the surface of an old, hand-built table. Edgar squatted, dug through his pack and found the small bag of corn. He pulled out a handful and sprinkled it on the table. Then, with a heavy sigh, he sank back into one of the two rough, straight-backed chairs. It was still early afternoon—and he wondered how long he'd have to wait before he had company.

He closed his eyes, and in moments had dropped into a light doze. Ignoring him, Grimm pecked happily at the corn.

# Chapter Nine

When Lenore and Anita set off into the swamp, Barnes took them across on the raft himself. He had a supply barge due that afternoon and needed to have the water and the dock clear.

"Your friend left early this morning," he said, poling across the waterway with quick, sure pressure on a tall, straight pole. He kept his eyes on the far bank and spoke matter-of-factly. "I thought the two of you might take off together."

"Mr. Poe has his mystery to solve," Lenore said. She had her bag over her shoulder, her drawing pad and a small easel. Her eyes were bright, and she stared into the trees ahead, as if she might pierce them and find what she sought without delay. "And I have mine. I have come a long way..."

Barnes didn't answer. He poled steadily, and within moments the raft bumped into the far bank. He held it steady.

"You'll have to jump ashore," he said. "I don't have time to pull up farther."

Lenore didn't hesitate. She perched on the edge of the raft, steadied herself, and leaped. She landed lightly on the bank and turned, holding out a hand to steady Anita, who followed her gracefully. Barnes tossed over the bag that Anita had brought with her—food and water and a few essentials for the day. They didn't plan to be gone more than that. The tree she sought was a couple of hours away, if they walked steadily. It would take her another couple to do her drawing, or, if it became too involved, the sketches she'd use to do the drawing that evening. They did not plan on being out overnight.

"You'll send someone across for us when we return?" she said.

Barnes glanced up at a tree behind her and to her right. She followed his gaze. On a lower branch, a large brass bell hung.

"We'll send someone. You ring if you need us."

Barnes pushed off, crossed the barge, laid his pole on the deck and began pulling the raft back across, hand over hand, by the mooring line. The small craft slipped sideways just slightly in the slow current, but that was fine. He intended to bring it in along the bank, rather than mooring to the dock, to make room for the supply barge and other traffic.

Lenore and Anita watched him for a moment, and then, turning with purpose, Lenore studied the three paths leading off into the swamp.

"To the right," Anita said.

The right path was the clearest, and obviously most traveled. It was wider than the others too, as if there might have been horse or cart travel along it.

"A lot of people go to the lake," Anita explained, shouldering her bag and starting forward. The fishing is good, and for hunters, the water draws the animals close. The path is clear all the way in, but once we get there, we have to travel a ways along the bank to reach the lady. We will pass the deer tree on our way."

Lenore had heard of the deer tree. She knew that when she saw it, she would feel compelled to draw it, so she'd planned ahead. She intended to do a quick sketch and embed the image in her mind, but to continue on to her destination. If the stories were true, the deer had already been there a very long time…a bit more would not hurt. The woman was a different story altogether.

The path was beautiful. The air was fresh, if a little humid. Butterflies flickered across the trail in their erratic dances, birds soared overhead and cried out, some mournful, others cheerful and bright. The voices of more types of frogs and insects than she could have imagined caromed off the trees. She listened for the sharp caw of a raven, but it never came. They were on their own, and no matter how close she now felt to Edgar, their paths had diverged.

Anita paused after about an hour, and the two shared a quick snack, a bit of cheese and bread, and a sip of good, fresh water. Lenore wished she could stay longer, draw the trees, and the wildlife. Her art had become so caught up in the dreams and images that she often felt drained, and the only way she'd found to regain her strength and focus was work that involved nothing more than her mind and her pencils, or pens, or paint. That was how the picture of Grimm was supposed to have worked. She'd only meant to draw the portrait as a gift to Edgar. Instead of granting her a mental and creative reprieve, the experience had drained her, leaving her with the sensation that her heart, and her mind, were a void, darkening and widening with every line or shade she created.

When this was over, she knew she'd have to find time away from it. Away from the visions and the art, away from the trapped souls and everyone who knew that she could see them. Even sitting in a city and drawing caricatures of passersby for change would be better than withering away to nothing.

"It's not too much farther, lady," Anita said, rising. "If we hurry, we'll get there just as the sun is at its highest, and the light is best."

Anita smiled and rose, following her new friend off down the path. She was not always this lucky. This trip she'd met Anita, Edgar, Grimm, and even young Tom, all of whom were supportive. More often than not, when her ability was brought to light, or she made the mistake of mentioning it, she drew only dark stares and furtive wards against the evil eye. It was a solitary road she traveled, and, like the art itself, the lack of companionship could be debilitating.

Sometimes it was even dangerous for her if she let her guard down. She'd seen a hint of it in the attitude of Barnes, the tavern keeper. If too many more odd things happened while she remained at the hotel, she would not only become unwelcome, but might be run off, or worse. They were a superstitious lot near the Great Dismal Swamp, and she did not want to provoke them.

They crossed a nearly open field, entered a tunnel of trees and broke through a moment later into a longer open stretch. In the distance, Lenore saw the glitter of water. The shore was skirted in brush, and though there were trees all the way to the lake's edge, or nearly, they thinned out the closer they approached. Farther back from the water, tall pines nearly blotted the sky. Those closer in were mostly cypress and willows, as if the lake formed a great bowl that stretched up and beyond its banks to the very uppermost branches of the surrounding forest.

By the water, the cypress trees were squat and oddly shaped. The roots formed small armies, tiny men or monks in robes, dragons and creatures crawling up and out of the bog. The willows dangled their trailing limbs to blow gently in the breeze. Frogs leaped from their perches to splash heavily in the water as the two approached, and at the base of one tree a dark water snake glared at them in open threat. Anita steered clear and worked her way right along the back. Lenore followed, taking it all in, trying to keep sketches in her mind to preserve the experience later. There was so much. She could have studied the cypress roots alone for hours.

They worked their way out around a patch of heavier brush, and as they turned back toward the shore, Lenore saw it. Caught in mid-leap, about five yards back from the shoreline, the deer was magnificent. The tree was a gnarled mess of cypress knots, moss, and mud, but the image was so clear that a small child would have seen it. There were shadowed holes where the eyes should be, the head was actually turned back to watch over its shoulder—the antlers rose majestic and alert. Trapped. It was a moment stolen from time, and as she stared at it, Lenore felt the reality draining from her world.

She backed away slowly. It felt as if the animal called to her, pleaded with her, as if it had dreamed of the day she would come and how she would set it free. Lenore shook her head.

"Not yet," she said. "Not now."

Anita had stopped, and, concerned, laid a hand on Lenore's shoulder. It startled her, and broke the spell. She backed away more rapidly, caught her foot on a fallen tree branch, and fell back, sitting abruptly in the loamy soil.

Anita cried out and hurried to help her up, but by the time she reacted, Lenore was laughing. It was absurd. She felt—and knew she looked—ridiculous. She'd known the deer would be there, and she'd anticipated her reaction. What she had not anticipated was its strength. The deer was a very old spirit, and still powerful. Its desire to be free had nearly overpowered her resolve.

"Are you okay?" Anita asked.

Lenore closed her eyes, ordered her thoughts, and nodded.

"It just took me by surprise. It's magnificent."

Anita glanced over at the tree. She saw the deer, of course, but Lenore knew that was where it ended, or, if the girl had some of the sight, it was nothing in comparison to what her overly-sensitive mind had picked up.

"I'll draw him later," Lenore said. "Tonight, maybe, or tomorrow. I've seen him—it's enough. I could never forget that sight. He almost makes you want to look back, as he is, as if whoever was hunting him was still out there, ready to track, and kill…"

"You are an amazing woman," Anita said. "I have been here many times since I was a girl. I have sat almost in his shade, around a fire with my brothers, frying the fish we'd caught during the day, laughing without a care. Now you come here—just the one time—and I see a completely different thing. I see a tragedy. I feel…pain. I have never sensed these things from the tree before. There really was a deer? A stag?"

Lenore nodded.

"A very long time ago, unless I've read him wrong. There is something more, too. Something…powerful. How many deer do you suppose were hunted on the shore of this lake?"

"Hundreds? Surely thousands. Why?"

"How many were able to turn themselves into a cypress tree and stand watch on the shore of the lake for generations?"

Anita turned back again and really studied the tree. She walked over, ran her hand over what would have been the animal's flanks. She shivered and stepped back.

"I see," she said. "Oh my God, I have been blind, I…"

"It is okay," Lenore said. She struggled to her feet, straightened her bags, and took Anita by the arm. "We have to go on. What we are about to do is more important still. We will not forget. I will not forget. He will be free again."

Anita nodded, but didn't speak. She turned, and very deliberately, she started off down the bank of Lake Drummond. Lenore fell in behind her, and as they put distance between themselves and the tree, the pressure eased. It was still there, she sensed him still standing—still watching—still calling to her, but it was a dim background noise. The waves slapping on the shoreline, and the cry of the birds overhead broke it apart and stole its clarity until, finally, she was focused on the task ahead once more.

They rounded another copse of trees, and the water curled back in on the land in a small cove. Across that tiny stretch of water, Lenore caught her first glimpse of the woman. She was not old, as she had expected. She was beautiful, and that was strange because in her dreams, the woman she sought blended her wrinkles with the rough bark of the tree, shared the gray of her hair with mist and reflected, silver moonlight. The sensation of immense age had been so clear.

Where the deer had been compelling and powerful, the woman was mesmerizing. The lake, the trees, everything surrounding them disappeared.

"We have to go around the water," Anita said. "You'll be able to see her better from there."

"I can see her just fine," Lenore said. Still, she walked around the bend in the water, ignoring roots and driftwood, oblivious to everything but the tree, and the image of the woman that it held. When she was very near, she glanced around, spotted a large stone sticking out of the ground, and walked to it. She sat, never taking her eyes off of the tree, and began to unpack her bag.

"Are you sure, lady?" Anita said.

"This is perfect," Lenore said. "I just need to set up my easel."

She turned and studied Anita.

"Will you be alright while I work? I may be here for some time and I'll need to concentrate."

Anita nodded. "I think I'm going to go back by the deer," she said. "After that, I may fish. I brought a line. It's been a long time since I was able to visit the lake. I love it here—so quiet and peaceful. Not like the tavern."

Lenore nodded. She heard the words, but was already falling into the vision, and away. The easel rested between her knees, and her sketchpad was propped on it, open to a fresh page. She reached for a pencil, pressed it to the paper, and began to draw.

# Chapter Ten

The afternoon passed quietly. Edgar felt as if he should be doing something, anything, but despite questioning Tom from every angle he could think of, he found no way through what was to come other than meeting Nettie, and no way to find Nettie other than to follow the stories he'd heard, and the odd ritual that lay ahead.

It should have seemed silly, sitting at a rustic table in the middle of a swamp, wearing another man's clothing, waiting with a bottle of homemade moonshine for an old woman who he believed could lead him to the lost princess from a fairy tale, who, by the way had been traveling with him for more than a decade in a raven disguised as a crow. Even he couldn't see a way to spin it into a story anyone would believe. Except that it was true.

The deeper the shadows grew, the deeper the chill that gripped his heart. Goosebumps stood out on his skin, and his brow felt clammy. He wanted to drink from his flask, but felt somehow that it would be wrong, that it might taint what was to come. He even looked longingly at the corn whiskey once or twice, wondering if sharing in the offering would compromise it.

Tom had retired to the cabin. He'd started a fire, burning low, but enough to light the interior. Surprisingly, the boy knew how to read, and when he'd seen the copy of Grimm's Fairy Tales, his face had lit up so brightly that, reluctant as he was to let the volume out of his hands at this point, Edgar had been unable to deny him the use of it. He'd pointed out a couple of his favorites, and handed it over.

The sun, which had warmed them so thoroughly during the day had hung over the tips of the trees for what seemed an eternity, and then, suddenly, dropped from sight, leaving a lingering reddish glow running down through the branches and underbrush. Everything about this place was slightly off-center from his experience.

He'd placed the bottle, unstoppered, in the center of the table. To either side of it were the small glasses he always carried along with his flask. The liquid was clear as water, though in the bottle it had had a dirty, yellowish hue, and the small tendrils of sunglow still left to the evening glittered through it, leaving a spot of light on the table that started out round and elongated moment by moment. Edgar watched it, fascinated. He concentrated, wondered how long it would grow before it was too dim to make out, or the light was too low on the horizon to create it. It inched closer, and, just as his sight blurred from the effort of convincing himself it no longer existed, he heard the sound of pouring liquid and sat upright with a start.

She was old. Her hair hung like silver silk over slender shoulders, and the garment she wore, not really a dress, but more of a tunic, draped loosely over a frame that seemed little more than bone. Her eyes, though, were deep and filled with mirth. She smiled, and, slowly, he regained his breath, and his wits.

"Brought an old woman a drink, did you?" she said. "Carried it out to me all this way. A fine thing to do. But why have you come, Edgar Poe? Why have you chased shadows into my swamp? There are no stories here. The dreams will not come."

"I...am not here for stories," Edgar said. "Grimm...the raven...carried a woman."

"Your familiar?" she said, watching him carefully for a reaction. "Where is your partner? Your guide? He flies by night, where no bird belongs—and he sees things you will never see. Why have you come to me when you are already bonded to such as he?"

"You know why," Edgar said. He saw that she'd poured two glasses, not just one, and he reached for his.

"She is safe," the old woman sighed. "I will protect her. Why do you follow?"

"There is always more to the story," Edgar said. "She did not turn herself into a crow, she was turned. There was another—a dark woman. She stole the girl, and all that was left was clues woven into a fairy tale. I do not know the rest of the story, but I have to believe that just because she has been freed, the telling is not done. If that dark one returned and stole the girl..."

"She must have had a reason," Nettie said. "And why do you need to know it? Why is this story anything more than a story to you? Why do you care?"

"Everything that has mattered in my life has been taken from me," he said, not sure why he told her this. "My wife is dying, and there is nothing that I can do for her. When I came to this place, I sought nothing but a new tale, something I could turn and twist to words, and to money. I could have gone straight through—they are expecting me. She is expecting me. Instead, I came here. And here..."

"Everything changed," Nettie said. "Yes, I know, everything changes. It's the way of life, of the world. Some things change, some remain the same, some seem to change and others deceive in their semblance of normalcy. You know this. Your words pull the strings in the deepest shadows of men's hearts. You will be remembered, Edgar Allan Poe. You will touch generations. You do not belong in this story."

"And yet," he said, "I am here, and there is no way out of a story except its ending. You are not the dark one. You are not the sorceress who captured the princess, and so, I wonder why you are here? Why do you protect her? What do you know that I do not know, and how can I trust that she is safe? She has been my companion, though I was unaware, and my dreams took me—Grimm took me—back. I may not have been written into the story when it was first penned, but that story was a diversion, and this—for all appearance to the contrary—is real."

"Everything we see, or seem," Nettie said softly.
"Yes," he said. "A dream within a dream."
"Drink with me, Edgar Poe," Nettie said.

And without really thinking about it, he did. The liquor was strong. He was used to cheap bar liquor, and watered drinks, but the bite of pure corn whiskey rushed down his throat like fire. The taste was earthy, with a hint of vegetation—a medicinal, chemical aftertaste, and a nearly blinding intensity. He coughed, but held it down, letting it settle and spread. He closed his eyes, fought for control, and as he did the world went dark. There was a sensation like air rushing past him, shifting through his hair and chilling his skin.

He opened his eyes, and realized he was standing on the edge of the swamp. There was no waterway, but somehow he knew what it was that he saw. It was a similar sensation to the dreams and images he shared with Grimm, but intensified. He took a step forward. The ground felt solid, and the sun was high in the sky, far from setting as he'd seen it do less than an hour before.

He heard a sound to his right and ducked into the trees. A moment later, three people appeared. One was a woman, tall, with dark hair. There were lines of silver running through it, but he could not determine her age. Her skin was smooth, but very pale. She scanned the trees with distaste.

Her companions were men. One was old, probably in his forties, and the other much younger. The two stood behind and off to either side, as if waiting for orders. Each carried a large pack, and both were armed with long, sharp blades.

"Here," she said. "We must enter here. We will have to find shelter, or make it. It will take time."

The older man nodded.

"Others may follow," the younger man said. "How far in?"

The woman tilted her head. She raised her nose and breathed deep. Then she turned.

"There is a lake," she said. "We will find the shore, and then we'll move inland far enough to remain out of sight. We'll have water, and there will be game. We must not be seen. Not yet."

"And she will come?" the younger man asked. He lifted his gaze to the trees, scanned the sky and the clouds."

"She is compelled," the woman said. "Wherever I go, wherever I lead, she cannot help but follow. Do you doubt me?"

She did not step toward him or raise her voice, but something in her tone caused the man to step back. He dropped suddenly to one knee and lowered his head.

"No, of course not. We will do as you bid. How far to the lake, lady?"

She smiled then, and Edgar had never seen an expression so devoid of humor, or emotion.

"Two miles, perhaps a little more," she said.

Then, without a backward glance, she stepped into the line of trees that bordered the swamp and disappeared. The two men hurried to catch up, and moments later, Edgar stood alone, watching the spot where the three had disappeared.

Then, like a shadow of what had passed, he saw another slight form. It was a girl—a young girl. On her back she carried a quiver of arrows, a bow slung over her shoulder. She moved so quickly and silently that once she'd passed from sight, he had to convince himself she'd been there at all.

Edgar took a deep breath, and, without considering the consequences, or wasting any thought on where he was, or how he'd come to be there, he followed them into the shadows. He'd come seeking answers—the only questions remaining were where had he come—when had he come—and how would he get back.

The journey passed in a flash, much more quickly than he knew that it should have, as time took another sidestep from whatever reality he'd been dropped into. He saw the three pass along the shore of a lake. He knew it must be Lake Drummond—there was no other so large in The Great Dismal Swamp. He was tempted to study the shore in search of the deer he'd heard of, or to watch the waves for sign of the Indian maiden's canoe. He did neither. He watched the woman, who was turning in a slow circle on the bank, as if momentarily confused. Finally she stopped and pointed, and the three set off toward the trees. Edgar was just about to slip out of his shadows and follow when the woman stopped short.

Facing her, just inside the trees, but clearly visible, stood Nettie. At least, the woman who stood there appeared to be Nettie. She leaned on a tall staff, and was flanked by a young girl. Edgar could not tell if it was the same girl with the bow and arrow, but she was certainly very similar.

The dark woman held out her hands to either side to prevent her companions from moving. She stood very still as Nettie stepped from the trees, stopped, and planted the staff in the soft earth. She regarded the intruders with a mixture of curiosity and distrust.

"What do you want here?" Nettie asked. She didn't seem to speak loudly, but her voice carried. To Edgar it sounded as if she were standing just behind him, out of sight. It made his skin prickle.

The dark woman took another step closer to Nettie. She stopped and smiled her empty smile.

"I have come a long way," she said. "I seek asylum. There are men following me, and I cannot let them catch me, so I have come here, to the swamp, to hide, and to rest."

Nettie cocked her head to the side, as if listening to a voice. She scowled, and then, unsmiling, returned her gaze to the dark woman.

"Who are you," she said. "Tell me true, and tell me all, or you will not be welcome here."

"They call me Estrella," the dark woman said. She took another slow step forward. She made no particular move that would indicate aggression, but Nettie stood suddenly taller, hands gripping the staff tightly.

"And as for my story," she said. "I have told you all that there is to tell. I have powerful enemies, and they will track me, if they can. I have run as far, and as fast as I was able. This is a place, I am told, where one can come, and hide, and possibly start over."

"Folks come here to hide," Nettie said. "Others come here to die, or be forgotten. Swamp is mostly a one-way trip. You will draw others, and still more after that. I will ask you one more time; tell me why you have come."

Estrella dropped her arms. She looked tired—defeated. Her shoulders slumped, but Edgar saw, at the same time, that a long, slender blade slipped from her sleeve into the palm of her hand. A second later, she was moving forward.

"Kill them," she cried, and the two men who accompanied her, blades drawn, darted toward the trees.

Nettie stood her ground, unperturbed. The girl dropped back a step, drew her bow, notched an arrow and let it fly so quickly that the older man was stumbling backward, the arrow protruding from his forehead, before he'd taken a full step. The younger man was quicker. He dodged to the right, dropped low to the ground, and scuttled forward, his sword held before him.

Estrella ran with the speed and grace of a much younger woman. As she moved, she seemed to grow. Her dress spread out like a gauzy cloud, like wings. She lost definition, shifted, and took on the aspect of a great bird.

Nettie stood her ground.

The girl flickered through the trees, stopped, spun, and shot. The young man swung his blade up, but he was too late. The arrow caught him in the throat, and he spun, falling back and away.

Estrella paid no heed. She had risen as she moved, spread and darkened, and with a cry like that of a great predatory owl, she dove. Edgar watched in horror. Nettie stood very still, and he saw, though he was too far away to hear any words, that her lips were moving. There was an odd, yellowish glow seeping along the ground at her feet. It rose to the trees behind her in a rush, and circled her in a sphere of brilliant light.

Edgar couldn't tell if that light was meant as some arcane weapon, or a shield against attack. It was clear that whatever it was, Estrella was not impressed. She dove like a dark streak. She struck the light, and it bowed, held, and she screamed again, pressing her attack.

Nettie smiled. She slipped out of the light just as Estrella burst through. For an instant, Edgar saw nothing at all. The light was so bright it nearly blinded him, and it spread, like a match dropping into a keg of kerosene. There was no sound. It was more of a sudden lack of sound. Air, leaves, branches—energy—all of it was sucked into the point where Nettie had stood.

Vines rose from the ground and whipped across that space. Trees bent double, their uppermost branches digging in like roots, and all the while the growing mass of light and vegetation contracted. A moment later, Edgar noticed that Nettie stood off to the side. She leaned easily on her staff, and she watched. The girl was back at her side. He glanced to where the two men had fallen. At first he saw nothing, and then he saw that there were raised mounds, strands of vines, tree roots, and weaving undergrowth. The mounds moved in a ponderous, relentless motion toward the trees.

Edgar shifted his concentration back to Nettie. The glowing mass had dimmed some, but he didn't think it was because the power had lessened, or even that the light had lost intensity. It was the swamp. It closed in over the top, formed a pulsing orb of green and darkness. There was a final scream. It was primal, filled with rage. As the light was fully encased, the sound was choked, until at last all Edgar saw was Nettie, an old woman leaning on a staff, the trees, and a snarled mass of undergrowth.

Nettie turned then, and stared straight at the point where he stood. His heart hammered, and sweat broke out on his brow, but she did not speak, or move toward him. Instead, unbelievably, she winked. Then she turned back and slapped the staff smartly against the vines and trees before her.

At first nothing happened. Then, like the splitting of an eggshell, a crack ran down the sides of the mound. It shivered, shook, and then huge clumps of it crumbled and fell away. Nettie stepped back. The outer shell dropped from the mound like sand pouring through an hourglass. When it was finished, Edgar caught his breath.

There was an old, gnarled cypress tree standing where Nettie had been scant moments before. There was no sign of the sorceress, Estrella, but the tree had a distinctly human shape. As he studied it, he saw the outline of her hair in the trailing vines, her outstretched arms, as if still diving forward to attack.

Edgar stepped from the trees then. He couldn't help himself. He started walking forward, and Nettie turned to meet his gaze. As he walked his sight blurred, and the world tilted. Dizziness stole his balance, and he toppled forward. He tried to raise his arms to stop his fall, but he felt heavy and sluggish. He closed his eyes and turned his head, readying himself for the pain of impact. It never came.

He raised his head and sat up straight.

The night had deepened. Someone had lit a candle, and the flame flickered, sending shadows dancing over the old wood porch. The light flickered over the glass of the moonshine bottle. The level of clear liquid had dropped considerably.

He turned then, expecting to find the chair across from him empty, but Nettie sat watching him with her eyes bright and inquisitive.

Edgar poured another small drink, trusting that it was not the liquor that had caused his vision. He tossed it back and closed his eyes for a moment before speaking.

"You captured her—in a tree."

It wasn't a question. He had heard the story of the woman and the tree, Lake Drummond, the trapped spirits that were so familiar to Lenore. This was only an extension of the knowledge he'd gained over the past few days.

"How long?"

"You do not want to know that answer," Nettie said. "If I told you, there would be too many more questions. What is important is that I knew why she had come. She would have lured the girl—and she would have stolen her youth, and her royal blood. If all had gone as she'd planned, she would have returned to rule in a land far from this place, killing, damning, and destroying all who got in her way. I read her—I judged her. This is my place. She should not have come."

"And now?" Edgar asked. "Surely her chance to rule has passed? The girl is safe?"

"As long as that dark one is trapped," Nettie said, "the girl is safe. Time has a way of bending and folding. I do not know what might happen if she were allowed to complete her spell. It does not matter—she is trapped."

Edgar tried to clear his thoughts. Something was bothering him. To buy time, he asked. "What about the deer? Did you trap the deer as well?"

He saw a flicker of emotion pass over Nettie's eyes then. Pain? Regret?

"No," she said simply. "He is an old…companion of mine. You will understand—you with your fine old bird. He drew too near to her—to my spell. She somehow found the power to twist what I had wrought, and she captured him. I cannot release him without setting her free. He would not want it."

Her voice had choked up at this last. Edgar slowly poured a little more of the moonshine into each of their glasses. He lifted his, and was about to ask another question, when it hit him like a stone to the head.

"My God," he said. "Lenore."

He didn't say another word, but as if his thoughts were nothing more than a book lying open on the table before her, Nettie gasped, and her eyes went wide.

"She will set her free," Edgar said. "She will not know what she is doing, but she will be compelled. She was drawn here by visions and by dreams."

"You have to stop her," Nettie said. "I will protect the girl. I can still handle the dark one, now that I know she's coming, but she will be more powerful. If she is reaching through my spell to draw others to the swamp, hiding their intent and their power from me, she has learned, and gathered her strength. You must be careful, and you must be swift. If you don't stop her I can still protect the girl—perhaps, I can protect you. The other—Lenore you called her? She will be lost."

The door behind Edgar swung open slightly, and Edgar turned. In that instant—the second his gaze did not fall directly upon her—Nettie disappeared. The bottle and what remained of its contents had also vanished.

"Gods," Edgar cursed. He rose, nearly toppling the table in his haste.

"We must leave," he said to Tom, who'd stepped confusedly onto the porch. "We must go now, and swiftly. I have to reach the banks of Lake Drummond."

# Chapter Eleven

Lenore had never felt such intensity while working on a drawing. She should have been done hours before. Normally, she would have settled for a fraction of the detail she'd already included, and still, even as she expanded the lines and shading, her pencil darted back to something that was not quite perfect, inserted a line here, or a shadow there that could be rendered with more clarity.

Anita had been back to check on her three times, but she had never even glanced up from her work. She felt the intrusion, and the shadow that crossed over the paper, but she could not draw herself from the trance the drawing had created. The lighting shifted as the sun rose to its zenith and dropped toward the horizon, but she did not falter. Though the shadows shifted, her memory supplied the details, and she drew, though her fingers were on the verge of cramping, and she feared if she gripped the pencil any tighter, it would shatter.

She knew that something was wrong, or, at least that something was different. When she had released spirits in the past, it had been a detached, very personal act. This was an entirely new experience. It had been her will that pressed her to the task, her stamina and talent against fatigue and time. She felt the shell of the tree crumbling as she drew, felt tendrils of thought working their way out to meld with her own. Whoever, or whatever, was trapped was taking an active part in the escape, and she didn't know if she approved, or if she should be fighting with every ounce of her strength, pushing the pencil to fail in its task, dragging herself up and away to run and run and never look back. In the end, it didn't matter what she thought; she did what she had come there to do. She drew, and her mind was filled with the image. It was all she could do to maintain surface control of her senses, and her actions.

She was beginning to pick up leaked thoughts and memories from the woman trapped in the tree. It was a wild rush of emotion. Hatred, pain, regret, frustration, and behind every bit of it an overwhelming aura of power and strength of will. Lenore tried to create a mental shield against it. She distracted herself by trying to insert other images, faces, remembering the words to Edgar's story as he'd told it.

That proved a mistake. As the words of the Brothers Grimm's The Raven wove into her thoughts, the trapped woman gripped them and twisted them savagely. The castle shifted from the storybook vision Lenore had constructed in her imagination to a stern, Gothic structure that almost seemed carved into the cliff side of a mountain. A road wound down from the keep toward a village below, obscured in wispy clouds of fog and shadows. There was a light in one tower window, and almost as if she'd been flung at it, the image enlarged and focused so rapidly it caused a sharp spike of pain.

She stared in through an open slit in a heavily curtained window. The hall beyond that window was large. There were squat, thick thrones set at either end of a long table that ran the length of the room. A man, presumably a king, or a lord, sat at the head of the table. Across the long expanse, a cold, haughty woman with thin, severe features sat—his queen? Behind, and to the left of the king, another figure stood. She was tall, slender, and very dark. Her hair, her eyes, even the robes she wore blended tightly to the shadows.

Lenore heard no voices, but the vision grew clearer with each passing second. The man finished his meal and rose. He waved to the shadows. The dark woman stepped forward, and then, from the opposite side, two men in uniform appeared, bearing weapons and armor. The lord held his arms out, and they dressed him for war, quickly and efficiently.

At the other end of the table, the woman sat staring in obvious disapproval. The dark woman leaned forward and whispered something to the lord, who nodded. Fully girded in chain mail, a great sword tucked into the scabbard at his side, he turned toward the woman at the far end of the table, who rose stiffly and approached. He reached out a hand, now gauntleted, and she placed hers upon it.

Sound slowly seeped into the growing clarity of the vision. As if from very far away, or down an echoing corridor, Lenore heard him speak.

"I will return before the winter is upon us. The borders must be defended. In my absence, your word shall be law."

The woman nodded.

"You will—or course—take council where it is proper. Estrella has been my eyes and ears in the village, and is a wise advisor. Trust her."

Again, the woman nodded, but as she did, she sent a glance toward Estrella that, had it been a solid blow, would have shattered her like glass.

"Is it only the affairs of the court that she advises you on, husband?" the woman asked. Her tone was light—devoid of emotion—but sharp as a blade.

He glared at her.

"You will do well to heed my wishes," he said. "Where is Adela? I would say farewell to my daughter."

"As you wish," the woman said. She turned and left the room.

Once she had departed, the dark woman stepped forward.

"She will never abide my council. I should travel with you. I could be ready in under an hour."

"You cannot. If you did, any suspicions she might have would be lent the weight of truth. I need you here to look after things, to be certain no harm befalls my daughter."

Estrella's eyes smoldered with frustrated anger.

"If you leave me with her, she will have her revenge. She is not so frail, or so innocent as you believe. I might be your advisor, but she is queen."

"You will do as I say," he said. "That is the end to it."

He turned then, as the queen returned with their daughter. He did not see the bright flash of anger that crossed Estrella's features, he had already dismissed her. In that moment, he only had eyes for the princess.

Adela was a small wisp of a child with bright blue eyes and hair that shone like braided gold. Behind her, a younger woman followed nervously, as if ready to throw herself to the floor and break the fall should the girl trip. Farther back the queen watched, her expression melting from disdain to hatred to anger, and directed at the back of her husband's head. Then she cast a glance at Estrella, and all indecision left her expression. Nothing but cold, calculated hatred remained.

The warrior lord dropped to one knee and engulfed his daughter in his arms. He leaned close, tickling her with his whiskers and after a few moments the girl was squirming and laughing. When he stood, he lifted her in a great hug.

"You will care for your mama while I am away, little one?"

"Yes, papa," the girl said. Then she giggled again.

Just for a moment, the hatred the queen directed at Estrella shifted to the girl, now tinged with jealousy. The king placed his daughter on the floor once more and patted her head, then turned to his wife. He tried to embrace her in the same way, but she stiffened, and though she returned his kiss, there was no emotion behind it. He stared at her a moment longer, then stepped away. Without a backward glance, he turned and strode from the room, the two guards falling in behind him, and only the women, the child's maid, and the little girl remained. The great door slammed with a booming thud.

No one spoke. The nurse maid gathered the princess into her arms, and backed out of the room. Neither the queen, nor Estrella spoke. After several moments of this, the dark woman bowed, and slipped back into the shadows, leaving the queen alone. When she was certain the others had left, the woman went into a rage. She dashed plates and goblets from the table, sent wine spilling in all directions, screeched like a banshee and finally crumple to a heap on her knees before the throne.

Then, very slowly, she rose. She composed herself. She left the room, and the image faded. Lenore felt a sudden rush of wind about her, and vertigo nearly caused her to pass out. Raucous cries surrounded her, and she saw the castle far below. Then, without warning, she dove. She tried to close her eyes, but was not in control of the eyes she used. The dive became a long, swooping circle, and then, with suddenness she felt should bring a sharp collision, but felt like a dropping onto a cloud, she stood on two long awkward feet, staring into the dimly lit interior of a different room—this one a tower chamber.

She had no time to reflect on the shifts in balance or perspective afforded by her sudden change. Within the chamber, she saw the woman, Estrella, and the little girl, Adela—the princess. The former paced the room, glancing anxiously out the windows at the night sky, the latter sitting quietly on the bed playing with a bit of ribbon.

Estrella crossed the chamber rapidly and pushed on the door to her chamber. It didn't open. She pounded her fists against the huge, solid panels, but they barely even made a sound, and they did not move. Leaving the door, she rushed to the window, directly where Lenore sat watching. She fought to back away, to drop off the ledge and take flight. She did not understand the mechanics of her new form, but felt the instinct of her host kicking in. She could not control it; it sat as if mesmerized, staring in through the window. Estrella's eyes blazed and she threw open the window, reaching blindly into the dark.

There was a cry from above. Like a ball of darker shadow, another winged form crashed onto the sill. It struck Lenore and she felt herself topple backward off the ledge. At first, there was nothing but rushing air, the sky above spiraled with stars, alight with the cloud-dimmed moon. Then whatever joined her to the bird and the story, the night and the wind failed with an audible SNAP and she was back on the shore of Lake Drummond. She realized that the snap must be the pencil she held, and she gasped glancing at the paper. It was fine. She'd pulled back, as the bird fell. She was no longer pressing the lead to the paper, and the drawing—the first stage was complete. She had the woman, trapped, all the nearly magical detail her talent could draw from lead and paper. All that remained was to set her free.

Except now it no longer seemed the proper thing to do. Her gift—her art—depended on changing the ending. She knew the story now—several versions of it—but the ending she was capable of providing, that where Estrella walked from the prison that had somehow been used to capture her, frightened Lenore more than anything had ever frightened her. She did not want to be the one to loose such a force on the Earth, or the swamp, her friends, or herself.

Fairy Tales, it seemed, could have their origin in reality, just like any other fiction. The problem with fairy tales was that they were put together in a formula that called for a great good, and a great evil, and what she had just created—what she intended, despite all her efforts to break free and turn her back on it, or destroy it—was to set that evil free.

She fought it. Before she could complete the ritual, she would have to unbind the image of the woman from that of the tree. She knew she had only one shot at it, and that if she could manage to mar the work, or destroy it, the moment would pass. It angered her to be drawn in, for her abilities to be shanghaied by some ancient evil that saw her only as a tool, or a key.

She heard a cry, far away and very high in the sky. She managed to turn her gaze from her drawing for a moment, but it was too dark to make out anything overhead.

"Lady?"

Anita had come close.

"I have to—finish," Lenore said, fighting each word, but unable to prevent herself. "We'll need to make a fire—get some light."

"We did not pack everything we need to camp," Anita said. "We have a little food, and some water…"

"The fire," Lenore said. "We'll be fine."

Anita stared at her for a long moment. Lenore silently hoped the girl would see the terror in her eyes, feel the change that had come over her and realize that something had gone wrong. If she had help—if she could somehow destroy, or ruin her work, there might be a chance to escape, to warn Edgar…and the girl.

Then Anita nodded, and turned away. As their joined gaze broke, Lenore prayed the girl would hear the soft pop as she did, and would turn back, but instead, Anita knelt, grabbed several pieces of driftwood, and began to build a fire.

Lenore turned back to the paper, dropped the broken pencil, and reached to her bag for her eraser. She listened, but, the raven's cry did not repeat.

# Chapter Twelve

Edgar tried to tell Tom what had happened, mixed up with bits and pieces of the original Grimm brothers Fairy Tale and the new version from his vision, but it came out in an unintelligible jumble, so he settled for galvanizing the boy into action. He had no idea how to get to the lake from where they were, whether they'd have to backtrack to the waterway and take the other path, but he knew they had to hurry. The sun was gone, and had been for some time. If Lenore had started drawing the minute she got to the tree, it was probably already too late, but they had a connection, and he still felt it—so he believed that it was not.

He heard Grimm cry out from far above, and he glanced up. The bird banked and circled, sliced down through the trees and landed on the porch railing. There was none of the restless shuffling, or irritated cocking of the head in the creature's demeanor. It met Edgar's gaze with an intensity that seared into his brain.

Tom banged out the door with their packs, hurriedly re-filled with all that had been emptied from them, and Edgar slung his over his shoulder.

"Where do we go?" he asked. "Can we get to the lake from here?"

"Sure," Tom said. "Folks who use this cabin come here to hunt and fish. We're not far, and I've walked there before, but I never done it in the dark."

Edgar nodded.

"Start us in the right direction," he said. "We have Grimm—he can watch to keep us on the trail. We have to hurry. We have to get there before she finishes. "

"Beggin' your pardon, Mr. Poe," Tom said, "but it's dark out now. How could she still be drawing?"

Edgar glanced down, thought about it, and then turned his gaze back to the swamp."

"I have spent the greater part of my adult life writing by lamplight or candle flame. If the work is not finished, she is still working on it, and we have to get there before it's complete. I have the distinct impression that if we wait until she is finished we'll know soon enough."

"We'll come out around the shore from her," Tom said, shouldering his pack and jumping down from the porch. "Maybe they'll have a fire to lead us when we get closer. What do we do when we find her?"

"I have no idea," Edgar said.

Tom turned and started off toward the swamp. Edgar squared his shoulders and followed. Grimm, without a sound, glided up to land on Edgar's shoulder, gripping the collar of his jacket.

The trail they followed was not as wide, or as well-used as the one they'd followed from the waterway. Gnarled roots snaked across the ground, fallen branches blocked the way. Edgar started slowly, having a hard time keeping Tom in sight, but as they progressed, he sensed something odd in their surroundings, something comforting and protective.

Though the ground was uneven, vines seemed to slither out of the way. Branches bent up or out—even holes and small ditches appeared to smooth as they passed. He sped his steps, and in a moment, though it brought a stitch to his side, and his heart to a hammering beat, he was running. Tom somehow sensed the right pace. He pushed, but not too hard, and he never got out of range, or left Edgar behind.

It only took a few steps of the jostling lurching run to send Grimm airborne. The old bird shot straight up until he cleared the tops of the trees, and then leveled off, pointing like the arrow on a compass to show where the path led. It wasn't necessary. Even parts of the path so choked with recent growth they would've needed a machete to clear them crumbled and fell away before them.

Though he had been more exhausted than he could ever remember being a short hour before, Edgar found that his pale, sedentary body performed beyond its limits. He'd have sworn, and would do so repeatedly at later dates, that he was feeding off of some energy source leaking up from the swamp through his feet. He felt years younger, and despite the weight of his pack, picked up speed the closer they drew to the lake.

He felt the nearness of the place as well. His senses were heightened by whatever aid Nettie was providing. It brought him close to the state where did his best writing, where the stories became part of him, the dreams molded themselves to reality, and he poured it all back onto paper to cleanse his mind. This night, it was not just a story—but the swamp itself.

There was no cleansing this. He sensed the lake ahead. He also sensed the presence of several others. One, he was certain, was Lenore. She drew him with warmth and life, but also with anger and fear, and again, he sped his steps.

There was a lighter glow that must have been Anita, pulsing, close, but with no particular power. Between the two he felt an immense darkness. It seethed and roiled, but was contained in a small area. It held them apart.

"Estrella," he breathed.

There was another. Some distance from the three, bright, as Estrella was dark, a fourth essence called to him. It felt different from anything he'd experienced. Then, as he grew nearer, he realized this wasn't absolutely true. It was unique, but not unfamiliar, because it reminded him of the bond he felt with Grimm—of the images and visions he shared with the bird, particularly in darkness, when he was working. Something was out there, and powerful as it was, it meant him no harm. In fact, he thought, if he could find a way to reach it, there was the chance it could aid him. Just a chance.

"How much farther," Edgar said, fighting to run and speak and breathe at the same time.

"Not far," Tom said. "I see a glow ahead—if there's a fire…"

Edgar didn't answer. He poured all that remained of his strength, concentration, and energy into increasing his speed. Whatever was going to happen, he would only be a part of it if he reached Lenore in time.

Grimm split the night with a great cry and began to circle, dropping at each pass, until as Edgar and Tom burst through the final ring of trees and onto the shore of Lake Drummond, he dropped to float just above the ground, looping back each time he pulled too far ahead.

Across the water, Lenore's fire was clearly visible. Edgar could make out a figure standing near that fire, and not far away, he saw the crooked form of an old tree. There were shadows huddled at the tree's base.

"Lenore!" he cried out as loudly as he could, and then, not wanting to waste any more breath, he tore off down the shoreline with Tom hard on his heels.

Lenore worked steadily. She was aware on one level that Anita stood nearby. She thought, very faintly, that she heard a voice from farther away, calling her name. Edgar? It didn't matter. She was focused, and trapped in the drawing, and her fingers flew over the paper now, erasing, brushing away the crumbs and erasing some more. Again, the experience of changing the drawing and freeing the trapped spirit had proven different.

Her normal method was to draw the trapped spirit and the object that imprisoned them, then to remove the trapped spirit, and finally to return to the inanimate prison—the drawing of that prison—to perfection minus what she set free. This time, it was different. She had no sense of the tree behind the woman. The two were inseparable, as if they'd never existed apart from one another. When all traces of the woman had been removed, there was very little left of the tree. Though her mind balked at this, her hands worked on—her fingers pressed the pencil to the drawing and she realized after a moment's horror what was happening.

She was recreating the tree as what it was—a prison. For it to truly exist, it required a prisoner, and she fought with every ounce of her being to prevent what was unfolding on the paper. It was a perfect likeness. She knew the image well, knew every crease and fold age had applied, how certain strands of hair would never stay in place, no matter how they had been restricted or styled. She knew the face as well as she knew anything on the Earth because it was her own. She was replacing the woman in the tree with herself and though she fought until the tendons in her arms felt as if they might snap, she could not prevent it from happening.

As the inevitability washed over her, she began striving to find something else, some way to divert the power that coursed through her and claimed her. If she could not free herself from this perversion of her talent, perhaps there was something else, some way to fight back that did not involve direct conflict.

She had already tried closing her eyes. Though she was able to complete the act, her fingers worked on, as sure and sound in their art as if she'd given her strictest attention. Now she tried something different. She relaxed her combat with the entity possessing her, and slowly turned her head toward Anita.

The girl was watching her intently, and when she saw Lenore's gaze swing to hers, her face lit with hope.

"Lady?" she said.

"Hurry…" Lenore croaked. "The deer. You must free it. No…time for detail. Draw it in the sand—the tree—erase the deer—set it free. Draw the…tree."

As whatever possessed her seemed suddenly to grow aware of the words, Lenore felt her gaze drawn back to the work at hand, to the drawing and its final details. She struggled to remain in control for a final word.

"Quickly!"

She tried to turn her head back, to plead with the girl with her eyes, to make her understand, but she could not. She sensed—or thought she sensed—Anita stumbling back. Then all she could do was work the details of the portrait unfolding on the paper, adding highlights, stretching out the act of creation by adding in more and more subtle lines and shades. If she could not prevent the drawing of this picture, she could make it perfect. She could make it take as long as possible to complete. She knew that the one part of her gift that could not be stolen was that moment of completion. If she could think of anything—any bit or piece of how the thing should look when finished—that had not been completed, she could delay that completion, and if she knew no other subject in the world well enough to play this sort of stalling game—she knew her own face.

Anita turned, and she ran. She had understood Lenore's message, and its urgency, but her heart hammered with doubt over what she might do. She had no gift, and she had no time. She had considered trying to drag Lenore from the fire, and the drawing, but the moment she recognized the lady's features in the tree, she knew she couldn't chance it. If things had progressed too far, who would be destroyed?

The deer was not far away, and it was close enough to the water that the sand was moist. She searched and quickly came up with a long, pointed branch that she gripped tightly. A voice—so faint she thought it must be wind in the limbs of the trees, or rippling waves on the lake—drifted to her.

"Clear your mind. See the deer. See the tree. There will be little time, but I can lend you strength. When I complete this drawing, I don't know what will happen to me, but I will have energy—strength—and I will lend it to you. What is in that tree—the animal, the spirit—it is important. It can help. You must hurry."

Anita did as she was told. She closed her eyes and listened to the night— the silence hanging over the lake and the crackling, blazing voice of the fire. She thought back to other times on that same shoreline, fishing with her brothers, studying the deer tree. It was almost a shock to realize she had done this, but now it seemed a part of the moment—something she'd seen in her own future beckoning, or some voice she had always heard there by the lake, just part of the experience that had slipped around her and become a part of her without any acknowledgment.

She knew this image. She knew this energy—this power. She opened her eyes, and, by the light of the moon, and the flickering flame of the fire, she drew. She had never tried before—never done more than doodle on the side of a paper while her mother taught her letters, or a scratching on the wall of the barn with a bit of charcoal. She had no idea what would happen—whether she'd end up with a childish stick picture of a deer, or...

The first line caught the swooping muscled shoulders. Her hand took on a life of its own, and she worked the tip through the soft sandy dirt quickly. Where it piled between lines she brushed it with her fingers, feathering it into shadows and dark highlights, moving faster and faster as she felt the energy behind her build. She fed off of it. Somehow Lenore channeled it to her, and the deer—the spirit—trapped in the tree joined itself to the creation.

Everything was funneling to a point. The drawing in the sand. The fire—the night—the power that flowed in and around and over her—the image that had trapped Lenore—all of it whirling like water into a deep hole, faster and faster until it was a blur. The deer came to life and at some point, a voice whispered—"Now...it has to be now"—and she stopped, beginning the act of dissolution—thinking strokes backward. She remembered her father taking her deep into the swamp when she was a little girl. She'd been afraid of being lost—afraid she'd never see home, or her mother again—and he'd told her to let the fear drop away. Think about what you did, and reverse it. Like flipping the egg timer, the sand flows one way, and then it flows back, always the same.

"You've taken all the steps, girl, just take them back."

And she did. One stroke at a time, she removed the deer. She didn't worry about the tree, she'd never seen the tree—but she had seen trees. She trusted her heart, and wiped the antlers, the flanks, the strong muscled chest from the earth. The time—the sand—had almost run out. She felt it approaching as if she'd dived from a cliff and saw the ground approaching ready to slam into her. That was the key—to ignore it—to time the completion so it coincided, and then—let it go. She had to let it go. She didn't know why, but she knew that she had to break all the connections binding her to the moment at that point, or be caught in it forever.

The deer disappeared, and with broad, strong strokes, she drew a tree. It was just a tree—a cypress—with gnarled knees and twisted branches. She filled space, severing all ties between the drawing she'd created and the tree she'd grown up knowing. Nothing existed but the need to reach completion.

Edgar's feet seemed to float above the surface of the shoreline. Never had he moved so swiftly, or with such purpose. After a hundred yards, he left Tom behind and continued to pick up speed. Each time his feet touched ground, his strength was renewed. His senses were heightened as well, and he quickly made out the two trees, the two women, and the fire. It was impossible to tell from so far off exactly what was taking place. He sensed some imminent event so crucial it could potentially break him into tiny bits and send him flying out over the lake, but still he ran.

Ahead of him, he saw Grimm gliding like an arrow, straight toward the farthest tree, and Lenore. It seemed as if he intended to dive straight into her, or into the tree. Edgar wanted to call out to the bird, or to form the now familiar link, but there was no time. He cursed softly and flung himself forward.

He was not going to make it to Lenore. Whatever Grimm planned, whatever else happened, the best he could do was to try and help the girl—Anita. She knelt, frantically scratching at the ground with a stick. He tried to concentrate, to figure out what she might be doing, but again, there was time only to move and to act. If he hesitated even for a second, he would become irrelevant to all. Instead, with an almost feral cry, he dove headlong, arms outstretched.

Lenore searched her memory for something, anything she might have left out—any part of herself she might add to the drawing and extend the creation. She found nothing. It was the most complete, the most amazingly accurate drawing she'd ever penned, and she was a single line from completing it. She wanted to glance over to see what Anita was doing, and she had heard Edgar's voice clearly more than once, though she had no idea how close he was, or what it would matter, in the end. She reached out with the pencil, placed it against the paper, and drew the final short line into the image.

As she did this, a huge, compressed burst of energy, power, anger, laughter, and so many other emotions and sensations that the intensity of it erased all thought from her mind burst forth. The tree shivered, and something huge, malevolent, and powerful dragged itself free. Lenore watched in fascination. The thing moved as if gripped by hot tar in a pit—dragged itself out of the wood and bark one limb at a time. It was vaguely shaped like a woman, but only vaguely at first. It was shadow, and that shadow was more concerned with freeing itself than with maintaining its earthly form.

Lenore screamed. It was the first sound she'd been able to utter since the vision had claimed her. She tried to rise, to turn and run, but her feet were rooted in place, and she was drawn up, formed, sculpted to the proper shape as she fought wildly—and futilely—with every thread of her being.

Something small and even darker than the thing climbing from the tree dove between her and what she'd set in motion. In, and then gone, so quickly, that Lenore only glimpsed a flicker of white as Grimm grabbed the drawing she'd made, bit into it with his beak, causing a tear, and soared off into the night.

The thing in the tree screamed as if that beak had torn into its flesh, but instead of slowing it, what happened next was final, dramatic, and horrifying. The creature—Estrella—shot up from the tree like a black flame. She poured over and out, shifting away from the curved limbs and torn bark, screeching in fury and wild laughter. As she tore free, shards of ice drove into Lenore's heart, and she snapped sideways, assumed the position of the bent old tree, and with a cry so soft no one but she could hear, winked out of existence.

Anita felt the end coming and drove the stick into the dirt. She joined two broken points on the image, completing her mind's creation—a tree with nothing trapped inside it; a tree with nothing but branches and leaves, jutting from the shoreline of the lake. She heard something, but could not make out what it was until—flying through the air like a crazy man—Edgar hit her, wrapped his arms around her and carried her on past the tree toward the water. There was a huge roaring sound, and what light the moon and the fire had lent the night was snuffed like a candle.

Edgar didn't hesitate. He rolled on top of the girl, clutched her tightly in his arms, and buried his head beside hers, keeping as low as possible, and not glancing up. He didn't know for sure what had happened, but he knew facing it at that moment would be the end of him, so he held very still, breathed in the scent of the loamy soil, and waited.

Behind, and to the side of him there was a splintering crack. He knew that it had to be the tree—the deer tree—but he couldn't turn to watch, or to wonder at what was taking place. Whatever had been freed, whatever was unleashed, let out a cry to match that of the initial burst of energy, and now—where the air had grown deathly cold and stale, there was a balance. On one side Edgar felt warmth—fueled by anger, but not by malice. On the other, there was nothing but shadow and rage, power and an unrelenting fury that prickled his skin as if he'd been pierced by hundreds of tiny needles.

"What can we do?" Anita said, trying to pull away.

"Nothing," Edgar said. "Do nothing, and be still."

He clutched her more tightly then, and closed his eyes.

# Chapter Thirteen

Miles away, Nettie raised her head. She had brought the girl to a safe place, a place where her power was strongest—where the roots of the trees and the soil had been joined for more than a hundred years. There was a sort of natural cave created by curving cypress roots and wrapped with vines and moss. She often came there to meditate, or to sing.

She had known the man would be too late. The events unfolding were long in coming, longer than most men or women had been alive. Nettie had lived many lives. Generations turned, and she was always there, along with the younger one. The Harvest brought the old magic to bear, and the great, horned creature she both loved and feared reared his head when he was called upon. It was as it had always been, before men, when the earth was one huge entity, not carved into swamps and forests, glens and fields.

Others had come and gone. She had known creatures and men, old powers, and new. She had remained—as she would always remain—guarding the land, protecting when she could—driving out the shadows. There was always new evil. The good wore away over time and was harder to replace, but the darkness swelled eternally.

The trap she'd created so long ago had held very well. It had served her, and the land, but all things change, and entropy was a strong taskmaster. Now the time had come for old confrontations to be renewed. She knew she had to protect the girl, if she could. Nettie had no idea where they came from, the dark lady and the bright, beautiful girl, but she knew they did not belong together. If left to her own ends, the sorceress would suck the youth from this one and use that power to fuel a revenge so cold those it was served upon would not even comprehend it.

Parts of Nettie remembered an older country. She was of this land, but her spirit—the belief that fueled her existence—had come from far away. The swamp had drawn them, and when they came, they brought her with them—her festival, and her bonfires—her dark, horned lover—the girl. All of it a cycle to be repeated as long as the hands on men's clocks ticked forward—and beyond. Time meant nothing to one such as she. She remembered a time when time itself was not even a fully realized concept. For her, all times existed. All the lives she'd lived were one.

She wove the vines more closely around the protective alcove and waited.

Then, something changed. Something unexpected—something she had not planned for and had no defense against. She heard the release as the darkness spewed forth from the old tree, but there was a second sound—a brighter break—a snapping of something rotten that revealed vibrant, brilliant life. Was it possible? How? Who could have freed him?

She rose and stepped away from the girl. She stood on the almost invisible trail and stared off toward the lake. She sensed the growing darkness, but there was another. Something stood against that shadow— something bright and pure and so familiar she ached at the deep, sensual psychic touch of it.

"Oh no," she said softly. "You cannot beat her. She will crush you. Alone, you will fall."

The woman let out a whistle, and then, simply, was gone.

From the weeds beside the trail, the young girl stepped out and turned, staring out the way Nettie had gone. She felt the conflict, but she was a creature of rules and discipline, strength and courage born of allegiance. Her place was here—to defend, and to guard. She was the vessel, and one day she knew she would see the world through other eyes. Older eyes. For the moment, she ducked in under the covering of vines and moss and drew them back over the opening, camouflaging herself, and her charge from sight. She didn't know what to expect, but it was not her nature to worry at such details. She would stay, and she would guard. All else would just… be. It was her way.

"The lady," Anita whispered. "She was by the tree. We have to go to her."

Edgar knew she was right. It was why he'd come. He didn't want to draw the attention of whatever dark force whirled above their heads, nor did he want to distract the other—whoever, or whatever it might be—that had squared off with the darkness. The tree—the now dead fire, snuffed from existence as if it had never given warmth, lay on the side of the shadows. It was all he could do to control his slamming heart, and to nod. He did so against Anita's shoulder, so she could feel him without the need to look up.

"'Stay low," he said. "Keep as close to the ground as possible, and as quiet. We will crawl. If we rise, or if that thing—whatever it is—notices us, I believe we will find that we would be better off dead."

They moved as quickly as possible, stopping every few feet, waiting, and then continuing again. Whatever was going on above and around them paid no more attention to their movements than a lion would pay a colony of ants passing alongside its den. It did nothing to change Edgar's certainty that if the focus shifted to them, it would be the last thing they ever worried about.

It took longer than he would have liked to reach the other tree. They had to skirt the small cove and the unnatural darkness made it more difficult still. It seemed hours before they turned back toward the water and started toward the tree.

They slipped past the fire, and Anita tugged on his sleeve.

"She was there," she said. She slipped her arm up between them and pointed to the stone where Lenore had sat, just short of the base of the tree.

They both stared.

"Where is she?" Edgar asked. He chanced raising his head and scanned the area. The pencils and drawing kit were scattered over the ground. The easel was collapsed in the dirt, and the pad lay across it, the top page flapping in the wind. He stared at it, but could make out nothing.

"It's a blank page," he said. "There is no drawing."

"That's impossible. She worked on it for hours. I saw it when she started. After a while, she couldn't seem to stop. She sent me to draw the deer…"

Edgar turned and stared at the girl. He'd wondered what had happened at the other tree. He thought back to what the old woman had told him. Now he knew—at least thought he knew—what was battling with the thing above them. He thought immediately of Grimm and wondered where the bird had gone. Then, before he could speak, he glanced up, and he saw the tree.

"My God," he said.

Anita rose up on her elbows and followed his gaze.

She was beautiful, possibly more beautiful than they'd ever seen her. Lenore's arm stretched up and out toward the lake. Her hair hung long and loose over her shoulders. One leg, bent at the knee, seemed almost in motion, as if she could run out over the waves and escape, while the other stretched back and down, blending slowly to the solid mass of roots that bound her to the soil.

"No," Anita said. Then she screamed it. "No!"

The scream ended in the deepest silence Edgar had ever known. He stood, not wanting to face whatever came next lying down, or on his knees. He stepped forward to the tree and laid his hand on Lenore's shoulder. He refused to look up, or in any way acknowledge the darkness swirling above him.

Anita stepped up beside him and also laid a hand on the tree. Tears flowed freely down her cheeks, and she leaned on Edgar for support. They stood that way for a moment, and then, as if waiting for just the right moment, a voice broke the silence.

"Lovely, isn't she?"

Edgar turned. The woman from his vision stood before him. She was dressed in the same dark dress she'd worn those many years before. Her hair was still dark, but the flecks of gray were gone. She oozed strength and power—it seemed to seep from her pores.

The sound of heavy breathing caught his attention, and with a great effort, he tore his gaze from the woman's and looked down the shoreline. Where Estrella was dark and willow-thin, the deer was golden, powerful, and magnificent. It stood, shoulders lowered as if ready to charge. One front hoof pawed lightly at the dirt. Its eyes glowed a deep, comforting amber.

The woman turned toward it and smiled. There was no mirth in the expression, no emotion at all.

"You have been dull company," she said, "and you will be an even duller opponent. I have known your kind, time and again. You serve well—you battle poorly."

"Maybe," a voice cut through the night like a hammer shattering brittle ice, "you should not concern yourself with boredom so soon. A wiser woman would already be gone from here with freedom so hard won."

Estrella spun snake-quick and actually hissed. The sound was the most evil thing Edgar had ever heard.

"You," Estrella said. "You dare to come here—after all that you have done to me, all that you have cost me."

"I cost you nothing but time," Nettie said. "You look well enough. I will tell you what I told you long ago. There is no place for you here."

"You have something that is mine," Estrella said flatly. "I will gladly leave if you return her. There is nothing left to hide from. When I return, those I knew will be nothing but dust, and I will be a nightmare tale told to children."

"You are already famous here," Nettie said. "You are the tree lady, the one trapped long ago by a power she could not withstand. The one who has watched over the lake for generations. They call you...tragic."

If Estrella was bothered by the taunting, it didn't show. She stood her ground almost placidly, staring first at Nettie, and then at the deer, as if deciding which was of more immediate danger to her.

"There is one missing," she said. "Where is your girl? She slew my men so many years ago, but she does not seem to be with you now." Then Estrella cocked her head to one side and studied Nettie carefully. "Or is she...I almost wish the two of us would have time to sit and talk. So many secrets, and so old. But I have places I must travel, and so..."

She struck like lightning. She flung her hand toward the deer and something dark—like glittering string—shot across the space. The animal was quick, but not quick enough, and the darkness twined around it, drawing in like a thick bag of energy and compressing.

"No!" Nettie's cry was high and keening. She launched herself toward the trapped deer, and in that instant, hesitating only long enough to turn to Edgar and actually wink...Estrella was simply...gone.

Edgar took off at a run. He didn't know if, or how he could help, but he saw Nettie reach the point where the deer had been trapped and grip the darkness, as if pulling on thread. He thought if he had done the same, it would have burned him, or dragged him in, but it did not matter. The only one who might help him—the only one who might know what to do about Lenore—was Nettie. He ran to her side, and heard Anita tight on his heels.

Before he reached her, Nettie turned to him. Her eyes were dark with anger.

"Stay back," she said.

She closed her eyes and grew very still. She reached her hands deeper into the still compressing darkness. The pulsing mass was alive with energy. Edgar felt the trapped creature inside, its emotion not exactly fear, but with a bright burning light of desperation, closing on madness.

Nettie did not move. She was so still she appeared to grow from the soil of the swamp, or to flow from the vegetation surrounding them, drawing strength from the air and deep cold waters of the lake. She turned her arms so that her hands touched in front of her, palms out to the sides. Then, with a whispered word and a quick exhalation of breath, she snapped those hands apart.

The darkness parted with a shivering explosion of energy, sound and light. Edgar and Anita were driven back, actually blown from their feet to land flat on the soft ground. The concussion robbed their sight, and their hearing. He tried to rise, but found that he was unable to move his arms, and that though his eyes were open, he saw nothing.

He tried to cry out then, to call for Nettie, or Anita, to scream his frustration, but even that release was denied him. Though he fought it with every ounce of his strength, darkness swirled around him and dragged him slowly down to unconsciousness.

# Chapter Fourteen

Nettie knelt on the beach and cradled the deer's head in her lap. He breathed, and with each passing second that breath grew stronger. She had closed out everything else. It had been so long. She had tried so hard, so many times to free him. She had lain at the foot of the tree to be near, and had drawn him into her dreams so they could roam the swamp together, but the pain was a constant, burning thing. She would never forgive the dark woman, or herself, for his entrapment. Now that he was free—now that he'd been returned—she could not bear seeing him come to harm, or worse, to lose him.

Now other things had been lost. Years spent working toward a single moment, only to cast the outcome aside for love. It was love, though not a type many would understand. The two were bonded—had been bonded—so long they were two parts of a single whole. Even the girl was not so close. Not yet.

That snapped her out of her daze. She had to get back. She did not feel as if the girl had been harmed, and she would know, but something had happened. Something had changed, and not for the better.

As the world came back into focus, she gently laid her old companion on the ground. Then, without rising, she pressed her palms to the earth and spoke a single word. The deer's eyes opened then. It lay still just for a second, then, rising in a swift graceful roll, it shook its head, tossing dirt and leaves from its antlers.

Nettie turned. Edgar and Anita lay side by side. She turned back.

"I must go," she said. "Guard them. It will not take long."

The deer's eyes glittered, and it slowly lowered its head. She reached out and stroked its neck, then turned, and, like Estrella, was simply not there.

The place where Nettie had left the girl—and the princess—was nearly destroyed. Despite her wards and protections, despite the age, and the central location—deep in the swamp where her power was greatest—great chunks had been blown from the roots of the old tree. A dark, smoldering patch stained the ground, and when Nettie peered inside, there was nothing. She turned then, searching the shadows, wishing, though she knew it was in vain, that the other was still present—that she could face her again and bring her down.

A sound to her left caught her attention, and she turned. The girl limped out from between the trees. The quiver of arrows on her back was empty. Blood dripped from the corner of her mouth, and the bow, snapped in the center, hung uselessly from her hand. Her expression had not changed.

Nettie went to her, supported her, and led her into what remained of the ruined chamber. She walked the girl to one wall, leaned her against it, and waited until her charge had settled. Then, stretching her arms over her head, she gripped the lower extremities of the roots. She began to speak, not words—at least not words any would have comprehended. The sound formed a cadence, and then a pulsing rhythm. From the ground at her feet, energy flowed up through her legs, her body and lit her eyes with a fierce, glowing brilliance. The burned and blackened roots flaked off their outer shell of bark and cinders and snaked out and down. Time sped up. Nettie fed the tree, and the swamp fed Nettie, and in only moments, the chamber was whole again—the vines had cut them off from the dying moonlight and the threat of day.

Nettie turned, sat in front of the girl, and waited.

"She came shortly after you left," the girl said, her voice soft, but steady. "At first, I thought she would not find us, but she sensed the other. I slipped out and tried to draw her away, but she paid no attention to me. I shot her then, twice. The first seemed to hurt her, but then—then she grew angry. The second she brushed aside before it touched her. I would have shot again, but she attacked. I don't know what it was. I was blasted into the trees, the bow..."

She held up the ruined remnant of her weapon. Nettie only nodded.

"She did the same to the wall that she had done to me. She burned it away and stepped through. The girl inside knew her, was afraid. I tried again to help her, but I could not. The dark one wrapped herself around the girl like a cloak, spoke, and then was no longer here. I searched, but nothing remains."

"You did what you could," Nettie said. "Did you hear what she said?"

"Rathburg," the girl replied. "Nothing more."

Again, Nettie nodded.

"Rest. There will be much for us to do in the next few days. I must return to the lake, but I will need you at full strength. When you have rested, tend to your bow."

The girl did not reply. She watched in silence as Nettie rose, slipped out into the rising glow of early morning that was seeping down through the trees, and disappeared.

Edgar woke to a throbbing headache that rendered him nearly incapable of coherent thought. He tried to sit, failed, and then on the second attempt managed to raise himself weakly. The first thing he saw was the deer. It stood before him, gazing down, and its eyes were as deep and dark as the swamp itself. Still, strange as it was, there was no malice in that gaze. Edgar nodded—hoping the animal would somehow see it as acknowledgment, or thanks.

He turned. Anita still lay beside him. Fighting rising nausea, Edgar turned, reached out, and gently shook her. At first there was no reaction, but he saw the steady rise and fall of her breathing, so he shook a little harder. Anita stirred after a few moments, raised an arm with what was obviously a great effort, and placed it over her eyes. Then, as memory and reason flooded back in, she moved the arm and tried to rise. Edgar shifted and got a hand under her shoulders, steadying her.

"Easy," he said. "That was quite an explosion—or—something like an explosion. Are you hurt?"

"I don't think so," she said. "My head hurts, and I'm dizzy."

The deer stepped forward then. Edgar turned, and it lowered its head. He shied away, nearly toppling Anita, who still lay across his arm. Ignoring him, the animal leaned even closer and softly nuzzled Anita's cheek. She stared up at it in wonder, then reached up and ran her hand over its muzzle.

"You're free…" she said.

Something passed between the two at that point, some shiver of energy and light. Anita sat up, shook her head, and then rose to her feet. She stepped close and wrapped her arms around the deer's neck, laying her head on his shoulder. Edgar could only sit, and stare stupidly.

"Don't you see?" Anita said after a moment. "The lady sent me to him. She knew he was trapped, knew that she would not get a chance to help him. She helped me—somehow she helped me set him free."

Edgar tried to stand, but before he got fully to his feet, dizziness swept over him, and he fell back to his knees. He was about to try a second time when he heard another voice, nearby, and behind. Nettie stepped out of the trees, crossed the sand, and laid her hands on his shoulders. She gripped him tightly, and the sickness drained away. He remembered how the ground had supported him on his run across the swamp, and that power and energy returned. When she stepped away, he rose, and the three of them stood on the shoreline in silence.

Sudden awareness widened Edgar's eyes.

"Tom!" he said. "The boy! Where is he? With everything that happened..."

"He is here," Nettie said. "He has been here all along. When the dark one burst from the tree, he ran. He is—after all—only a boy. He hid in the swamp, and he stayed there, afraid for his life—but unwilling to leave you here alone. I found him on my way in, sleeping. He will be fine."

"Grimm?" Edgar asked. He scanned the sky over the lake, checked the trees, but saw no sign of his feathered companion.

"I do not know," Nettie said. "I can tell you that your bond would tell you if he'd been harmed. I did not see his part in what took place, and though I sense he was here, and that he acted, I do not sense him now. He will return."

Edgar turned to the lake and stared out over it. He knew that what she said was probably true. Grimm had left at other times, and returned, but somehow this felt different. There was a dark, empty void in the hollow of his chest. He did not believe it could all be attributed to Lenore—he needed his companion.

"Lenore," he said. "You know what happened?"

Nettie nodded. They all walked toward the tree that, for so long, had trapped Estrella on the banks of the lake. The shape of the tree had not changed so much, just the lines, and the features of the woman trapped inside. They were much clearer than they had been, less crude. The tree had the aspect of a great sculpture—an uncanny, unbelievable likeness.

Edgar laid his hand on one of the branches, then pulled it back suddenly—his eyes wide.

"I felt..."

"Her," Nettie said. "She is there. She knows we are here—senses us. She cannot reach out to you, but she knows that we are near."

"What is this?" Anita asked.

She knelt beside the tree and ran her finger down the trunk. A jagged crack ran from deep beneath the ground up into the trunk. It fell just short of where Lenore's knee began. The girl turned her face up to meet Nettie's gaze.

"I'm not sure, child," the old woman said.

She squatted and stared at the crack intently.

"There was no such crack before," she said. "Something caused this—something interfered at the last moment. The dark one would not have left anything to chance. This...opens possibilities. I do not believe that I can free her. This tree—it is not my tree. That one burst asunder. But the roots will not be as strong—because it's my land. I will keep it safe, and I will study it. If I can—I will free her."

Anita turned back to the tree.

"She showed me how," she said. "I could draw her...I could set her free..."

"No!" Edgar said. He didn't know why this thought frightened him, but it did. "It's not the same. This is not one of her spirits trapped on the way to the next life—it is a trap. You see what happened when she freed the sorceress. Lenore became trapped, and the same, I'm afraid, would happen to you. She would not want that—she would be horrified. We have to find another way."

Nettie was still staring at the crack, lost in thought.

She turned to Edgar.

"I think your bird will know," she said. "At least, I think he had a hand in...this."

She bent and ran her hand over the crack, probing.

"What about the princess?" Edgar asked. "The girl Grimm carried so far. Where is she?"

"Gone," Nettie said.

Edgar wanted to push her for details, but her humor seemed to be slipping, and he did not want to push his luck. He did not want to be on her bad side. He glanced up the shore and saw Tom climbing out from behind a log. The boy was rubbing the sleep from his eye, trying not to look directly into the sun rising over the treetops.

"We can't just leave her," Anita said.

Edgar's expression darkened, all humor draining from him in the span of an instant.

"We cannot stay here," he said. "There is nothing we can do. We will try to find a way, but for now..."

"You must leave." Nettie concluded. "There has been too much darkness here. The lake—the land—the swamp—we must all heal. She is safe," she laid a hand on a branch of the tree. "I, or one of mine, will come here daily. We will sit with her. She will feel our presence. I will not leave her alone."

"I will come, too," Anita said. "I can sense her as well. I will learn what I can—the drawing. If I cannot free her, there are others. So many…"

Nettie stared at the girl, as if weighing her against some inner standard, then nodded. "You will be welcome," she said. "There are things I can teach, as well. There are other worlds than these and in some—the walls are thinner. Perhaps you and the one you call Lenore shall meet again on a different shore."

Tom stumbled up to them in time to hear these last words. He looked at each of them in turn, confused. After a moment, Edgar smiled—though it was a thin, pallid attempt at it, and reached out to ruffle the boy's hair.

"Did you sleep well, then?" he asked. "It seems a lot has happened since we tried to kill ourselves running through the swamp."

Tom looked sheepish.

"The last thing I remember is following you as you ran to the deer tree. Something happened then, like the earth just exploded. I turned tail and got out. Guess I fell, and…well…that's the last thing I remember."

"I think," Edgar said, "that this one time you can be glad to have lost a few hours. They were not good ones for any of us. Well…not for most."

He turned to where the deer still stood nearby. Tom followed his gaze and the boy's eyes widened. Amazed, he took a step toward the animal.

"It's okay boy," Nettie said. "He won't hurt you. Fact is, I sense you've spent more than a few days in his company. He seems to know you."

Tom walked slowly up to the deer and held out his hand. The animal leaned down and rested the side of its head on his palm. Tom shivered, and when he turned back to the group, his eyes danced with wonder.

"I…I feel him…in my head. He's…"

"Wonderful." Nettie said. "He has been my companion for so many years the world has lost count. He is—similar—to the raven. Older, I think, and a bit more powerful."

"Lenore called them—familiars," Edgar said. "I had thought the term only applied to witches…"

"And what are you then?" Nettie asked, turning to him and raising an eyebrow. "What would you call a man who dreams and then, when he records those dreams on paper, changes the world? What would you call a man who sees events so far away in time and miles that he unravels the secrets behind fairy tales? You are a writer—you have a magic of your own. Never forget that words, and names, have power."

"I have never doubted the magic," Edgar said. "For all the good it has done me. I came to this place to write, to try and forget the world, where my wife lies dying, and instead of solace, I have lost another—perhaps two—and gained nothing but a new story, should I choose to write it. You'll forgive me, lady, if I am underwhelmed by my gifts that, while able to grant me peace in small quantity, seem absolutely unable to help those that matter to me."

"You have helped me, Edgar Allan Poe," Nettie said. "It is a debt I will not soon forget, and worth more—I think—than the story. You must learn patience."

"If I had the years to learn that lesson that you have had, lady," Edgar said, "I believe I would be quite mad. It was my pleasure, and my honor, to have helped in any small way."

"Remember what I said about worlds," Nettie said, "and time. You have said it yourself—I heard it like a whisper on the wind. It is all dreams within dreams. That is the real secret. Time is not made up of one long string, but of layers."

"You didn't say that," he said softly. "Lenore did. I pray that she was right. Of course, more than ever I'm uncertain in which direction to aim that prayer, or if I should expect an answer, or create my own."

He turned to Tom. "I don't suppose you know where we dropped our bags? I'm suddenly quite hungry, and we will need to start on our way back soon. We'll have to have a story—they will want to know what happened to Lenore. They are unlikely to believe the truth."

"One thing," Nettie said. "Before I go—there is something. Before the princess was taken, the girl heard the dark one speak. A single word. I believe it's a place, an old world place, but it may also be a clue. She said 'Rathburg.'"

"Rathburg," Edgar repeated. "I'm not familiar with the name, but it sounds as though it might be a German name. For some reason—it makes me think of mountains."

"It is all that I have," Nettie said. "Now, the sun is up, and I am very, very weary. I must go, and you must leave as well. If it will help, I can arrange for evidence to support an attack by a bear. There will not be much to go on, but if you tell the story well—and something tells me that is not a problem for one such as yourself—they will believe. They will want to believe, because it's a story that does not threaten their world. They may notice that the tree seems different—but they won't know in what way. I will regrow the deer tree, in my companion's honor. There will be nothing trapped within it, or in any other part of my domain as long as I can prevent it."

Tom had run off, and now returned dragging the two packs behind him. They were a bit worse for wear, and the bedrolls were gone completely, but for the most part they seemed intact. Edgar took his, opened it, and fished around inside. He came up with his flask, and he smiled. When he turned back to the others, Nettie and the deer were gone. Anita stood, staring back at the tree—now a prison for one they had both, in a very short time, come to love. Tom was fishing food from his own pack. None of them had seen the old woman go—but they were quite alone.

He saw that the deer tree, or something very similar to the tree that had stood there before, had returned. All evidence of the blast of power, the fire, all of it had vanished. Anita walked over to the tree and knelt once more. She carefully gathered the pencils, the eraser, and all of Lenore's possessions. The bag that had held them still lay where Lenore had placed it, and she packed it all away carefully.

"I will talk to Barnes," Edgar said. "I believe she would have wanted you to have what was hers. I doubt there is anything of too much value, but what there is…"

Anita nodded, but could not bring herself to speak. She rose, and stood staring into the smooth, wooden features embedded so perfectly in the lines of the old tree.

"I found this," Tom said.

They turned and saw he held out slices of jerked meat. Each of them took one, chewing unenthusiastically.

"There's not much water," he said, "but we can share what we have. We should start back."

Edgar nodded. Anita looked, just for a moment, as if she might not follow. She stood close by the tree, her hand on a branch and her eyes closed. Then she stepped back, turned, and started for the trail leading back to the waterway, and the tavern beyond.

None of them spoke, and it seemed even the creatures of the swamp remained silent as they passed into the shadows of the trees.

# Chapter Fifteen

In the end, their story wasn't questioned at all. Barnes gathered a party of hunters to return to the lake and try and track the bear. They found tracks, and they found what might have been human remains, though not enough to truly identify the body. No one doubted them. They were exhausted in mind, body, and spirit, and it was easy to modify their shock and loss into a story that made sense.

Barnes was quick to agree to let Edgar take possession of Lenore's belongings. He was already spooked by the strange happenings in and around his roadhouse, and more than happy to be rid of anything that might remind him. He seemed relieved when Edgar said that he could only stay a few more days.

"I have to tell you, Mr. Poe," he said, "things haven't been right since that woman came to stay, and they only got stranger on your arrival. I hope you won't think me rude when I say I'll be glad to see the south end of it all headed north, if you take my meaning."

"I will be glad to be on the road as well," Edgar said. "I've been too long away from my home, and this tragedy has only made the separation more painful. I still have a bit of work to complete, but when that is done, I will take my leave."

"There's a coach in three days," Barnes said. He didn't look up from where he was polishing the bar, but the message behind his words was clear enough.'

"I will endeavor to be on it, then," Edgar said.

Anita had waited in Edgar's room, resting on the bed as he discussed things with Barnes. She had not returned to work; she needed time to recover. She had also not gone home. Edgar walked with her to Lenore's quarters, and together they gathered up the few belongings left behind. Edgar took the portrait of Grimm and rolled it tightly. There were other drawings, but these he left with Anita.

"You can study them," he said. "Perhaps you can sell a few—you will need supplies, if you intend to follow in her footsteps."

"I don't know what I will be able to do," she said. "I know that I must try. And I will spend all the time that I can by her side—though it will be a while before they allow it. With a 'killer bear' on the loose they will be vigilant. Also, I will have to convince my family—and Roberto. I don't know how I will explain this, but I know that I must find a way."

"Will you do something for me?" Edgar asked.

"Of course…"

"The boy, Tom? Keep an eye on him? Make sure he finds time to learn— to read, to write—that he isn't forgotten? He has done me a great service— all of us, really. Without him I'd have been lost as surely as I breathe."

Anita smiled.

"That is an easy thing," she said. "He's a good boy, and so long as Mr. Barnes keeps us both employed, I should be able to find time to spend with him. None of us is quite the same now, you know? What happened—that kind of thing sticks with you. I believe he has ideas of slipping back into the swamp himself. He was very taken with the deer."

Edgar thought about this.

"I don't know if it is a good thing, or a bad thing, to seek out Nettie," he said. "I do know that if she had not been with us, we would likely all be dead."

"If you had not knocked me to the ground when you did," Anita said, "I would be dead for certain—or worse, trapped in that very tree…"

"So many things that might have been," Edgar said. "My life—I'm afraid—will be recorded as a series of things that are, and better things that might have been. My heart is sore, and I have never felt so weary."

"I should go," Anita said.

She gathered up Lenore's things, and they walked to the door. Edgar locked the room behind them and turned back toward the tavern.

"I will return the key," he said. "You go on. Your family will have heard rumors by now of the bear, and the attack. They will be worried."

Anita nodded. She stepped forward, then, impulsively, stood on her toes and kissed Edgar on the cheek.

"Goodbye, Edgar Allan Poe," she said. "I will watch the magazines and books that come through the tavern for your name, and your stories."

"And I will watch for all of you," he said, "in my dreams."

Then she turned and hurried off down the road into North Carolina, and Edgar turned away. He returned Lenore's key to Barnes, and then locked himself in his own room, pulled the shade, and without even stripping off his clothing, lay back on the bed and fell into a deep, dark sleep.

In his dream, he sat in a chamber overlooking a shadowed valley. The room was a library, heavy leather bound tomes lining dark oak shelves, tapestries strung on the walls, and in one corner, an immense desk with a brass lamp. He walked along the shelves, pulling out one book, and then another, fascinated by the titles, though they slipped from his mind as soon as he placed them back on the shelf.

The room felt comfortable, and that was strange, because though he knew every inch of it, he also knew that he'd never been there before. The details came to him as he needed them, but then, as each moment passed— they slipped away. There was a sound, like someone rapping gently on the door. He crossed the room and opened the door. There was no one on the other side, and he was about to close it, when something dark and fast flew at his face. There was a flutter of wings, and a loud squawk. Edgar stepped back, surprised, but when he turned, it was Grimm he faced, standing on the edge of the great desk.

The bird held something in his beak, and Edgar crossed over to pull it free. He held it up, and his heart nearly stopped. It was a drawing, possibly the finest drawing he'd ever seen. It was Lenore, the way she'd been when he saw her last, blending to the lines of the tree. At the base of the drawing, the paper was torn.

Edgar glanced up, measured it quickly against Grimm's beak, and he knew.

"She isn't getting out of that tree, old friend," he said. "She's trapped. You made a crack in the armor, but it held. The old woman will try, but..."

He stared at the drawing, and was surprised at the tears trickling from the corners of his eyes. He remembered how Lenore had preserved the other drawing, the one of Grimm, and he did as she had done and then rolled it carefully until it was a tight tube. He walked to the desk and opened the center drawer, knowing there would be a ribbon there, and again, not knowing how he knew.

There was a coat tree by the door, and on it a floor-length black jacket hung. Above it, on another hook, was a black felt hat. Edgar took the jacket and swung it on over his shoulders. He tucked the drawing into an inner pocket, and—almost as an afterthought—he grabbed that hat and settled it on his head. Both jacket and hat were a perfect fit. He glanced over his shoulder.

"It's never going to be the same again, is it?" he said.

The bird regarded him gravely, and then, in a voice somewhere between gravel grinding together and leaves rustling over the ground, he spoke.

"Nevermore," he said. "Nevermore."

As Grimm lifted off from the desk, gliding to his shoulder, Edgar turned and opened the door. They stepped into perfect darkness and—with a start—he woke.

He sat up in the bed, still dressed, and looked at the window. It was dark. He rose and crossed to the table. After a moment, he had the lantern lit. He turned up the wick so the glow spread over the table and out toward the corners of the room. He turned, and then he stood very, very still.

On a hook by the door, a long, dark coat hung. On top of it, perched at a jaunty angle, the hat. He turned, and glanced up to the mantel. Grimm watched him so intently he would have sworn the old raven was getting ready to fly to safety if he reacted incorrectly.

"What have we done?" he said softly. "My God."

He crossed quickly to the jacket and slid his hand in around to the inside pocket. He felt the rolled drawing. He did not pull it out. Instead, he returned to the table, reached beneath, pulled free his bag, and brought out the flask, his sheaf of blank pages—and his pens. Grimm glided down to rest on the back of the one other chair in the room and watched him closely.

Edgar unscrewed the lid on the flask, took a long pull of the liquor, then capped it and set it aside. He opened his ink, dipped his pen, and turned to the first blank sheet of paper. His mind slipped back to the swamp and to that room—the library he'd never visited—where he now belonged. He pressed the quill to the paper, and began to write:

"Once upon a midnight dreary, while I pondered, weak and weary,
Over many a quaint and curious volume of forgotten lore—
While I nodded, nearly napping, suddenly there came a tapping,
As of someone gently rapping—rapping at my chamber door…
"Tis some visitor," I muttered, "tapping at my chamber door—
Only this, and nothing more…"

He wrote on into the night, as the candle burned slowly through its well of oil and the moon made her nightly crossing of the heavens. Grimm did not speak, but Edgar heard the voice in his head.

Over the next few days, he wrote the verses several more times, changing them, erasing bits and pieces of what was true, and replacing them with images he thought others might relate to. It helped to ease the pain, diluting the story and reworking the rhymes. It reminded him of the Brothers Grimm, and their fairy tales, obscuring truth in clever turns of phrase. He ate in the tavern, sitting at the same table he'd so recently shared with Lenore.

Once or twice, Anita or Tom joined him. Anita had taken to carrying a small pad of paper with her everywhere she went. He'd seen some of the sketches she was working on, and while they lacked the technical surety of Lenore's work, they were very good and getting better.

Tom was quiet. He'd spent a good deal of time across the water in the swamp. He'd guided a couple of parties trying to find the bear that had 'killed' Lenore, but Edgar knew the truth. He was watching for Nettie, or the deer. He was thinking about the girl with her bow. Edgar suspected that when the time came to choose this year's Harvest Lord, Tom would be doing anything he could to be their first choice.

And finally, rested, and restless, the time had come to depart. The carriage passing through to Virginia would stop early in the morning, and Edgar found himself with one final night in the tavern.

He seated himself early and enjoyed a meal of stew and hot, fresh bread. He didn't ask what was in the stew, and offered a silent prayer that it wasn't venison. As he ate, he watched the trees beyond the window. No faces were evident, and he saw no strange lights or figures. He was almost sorry.

He ordered whiskey, and asked Barnes to leave a bottle at the table. The melancholy was settling around him like a shroud, and he knew sleep would not come soon, or easily.

About an hour after dark, the doors opened, and a man walked in that Edgar had never seen. He was a young man, very tall—more than six feet—with long, dark hair pulled back over his shoulder and tied in back. He wore a floor length black coat that gave Edgar a start. Just for a second, he thought it was his—the jacket from his dream. The man's eyes flashed as they caught a glimmer of lamplight, and Edgar would have sworn they glowed a dim violet.

The stranger scanned the room, and when his gaze fell on Edgar, it rested there. The young man smiled, an enigmatic, curious expression, and slowly crossed the room. It wasn't until he had nearly reached the table that

Edgar noticed the cat pacing along at his heels. It was a strange animal, spotted, larger than any housecat Edgar had encountered.

The two reached the table. The young man gave an odd bow, and held out a hand. His cat, without hesitation, jumped to one of the chairs near the wall and curled into a ball.

"Good evening," the stranger said. "My name is Donovan. Donovan DeChance. I'm afraid I don't know anyone here, and…I don't know why, but you have an air of familiarity—as if I should know you."

"Edgar. Edgar Poe. I don't believe that we've met, but you are welcome to share my table. It can get busy, and a little rough, depending on the crowd. Your cat seems already to have made herself at home."

"I'll confess that's another reason I felt I had to introduce myself. She isn't generally friendly to strangers."

"Have a seat Mr. DeChance," Edgar said. "Have some whiskey. It's my last night here, and I was feeling a little down. It's been an odd week, and I could use some company."

DeChance made his odd bow again, and sat across the table, facing Edgar.

Then, with a smile that was oddly engaging, he poured them both a drink from the bottle on the table, and leaned back.

"I'm not sure why," he said, "but I have the strangest urge."

"What on earth could that be?" Edgar asked.

"There is something about you," Donovan said slowly, "that tells me you would tell a good story. Something with magic, romance, something different to erase the dust of the road."

Edgar stared at him. Beyond the man's shoulder, a dark, winged form shot past the window, circled back, and came to rest on the sill. Donovan glanced back, nodded, and returned his attention to Edgar.

"In the swamp," Edgar began, "there is a lake. They call it Lake Drummond, and I'm told it has deep, dark secrets to share."

"Told?" Donovan said.

"All stories," Edgar said with a smile, "Begin with a grain of truth; even our dreams."

The stranger sat back and sipped his drink, and Edgar began to talk. The moon had risen to her throne in the center of the night sky and begun to dip to the horizon by the time he'd finished. When he was done, he pulled a folded paper from the pocket of his shirt and handed it across the table.

"That was…remarkable," Donovan said. "What is this?"

"I'll ask you not to read it until I have gone," Edgar said. "It isn't a final copy; I still have work to do. Some truth requires several veils before being revealed to the world. Sometimes even the veil is insufficient."

Donovan did not question this. He tucked the paper into the inside pocket of his jacket, and he stood.

"I am glad to have met you, Edgar Poe," he said. "It was an amazing story, filled, I believe, with more grains of truth than most. It is tragic, and shows a flair for the dramatic sorely lacking in much American literature. I suspect that I will see your name again."

"If you are ever near Philadelphia," Edgar said, "You must look me up. You owe me a drink, after all."

Donovan nodded, and bowed. Edgar, without realizing he had done so, mimicked the gesture, then stared at his companion thoughtfully.

"Have a good journey, Mr. DeChance," he said. "Perhaps when next we meet you'll tell me a story. I believe you must have a bit of the magic about you as well, and I do love a good tale."

Edgar laid a handful of coins on the table, turned, and left the tavern. When he reached his room, he considered sitting and writing, but decided—this once—that he'd told all the stories he needed to tell. He undressed slowly, and prepared for sleep. A rapping on the window announced Grimm's arrival, and he let the bird in.

Then—for the first time in his recent memory—he put the world out of his thoughts and settled back on the bed. He slept without dreams.

# About the Author

David Niall Wilson has been writing and publishing horror, dark fantasy, and science fiction since the mid-eighties. An ordained minister, once President of the Horror Writer's Association and multiple recipient of the Bram Stoker Award, his novels include Maelstrom; The Mote in Andrea's Eye, Deep Blue; the Grails Covenant Trilogy; Star Trek Voyager: Chrysalis; Except You Go Through Shadow; This is My Blood; Ancient Eyes; On the Third Day; The Orffyreus Wheel; The DeChance Chronicles, including Heart of a Dragon, Vintage Soul, My Soul to Keep, Kali's Tale and the soon-to-be-released Nevermore; The Parting and The Temple of Camazotz, both for the original series O.C.L.T.; and the memoir/cookbook American Pies: Baking with Dave the Pie Guy. David can be found at http://www.david-niallwilson.com and can be reached by e-mail at david@macabreink.com.

David is CEO and founder of Crossroad Press, a cutting edge digital publishing company specializing in electronic novels, collections, and non-fiction, as well as unabridged audiobooks and print titles. Visit Crossroad Press at http://store.crossroadpress.com

Curious about other Crossroad Press books?
Stop by our site:
https://www.crossroadpress.com
We offer quality writing
in digital, audio, and print formats.